SATURDAY NIGHT SPECIAL

WILD IRISH, BOOK 6

MARI CARR

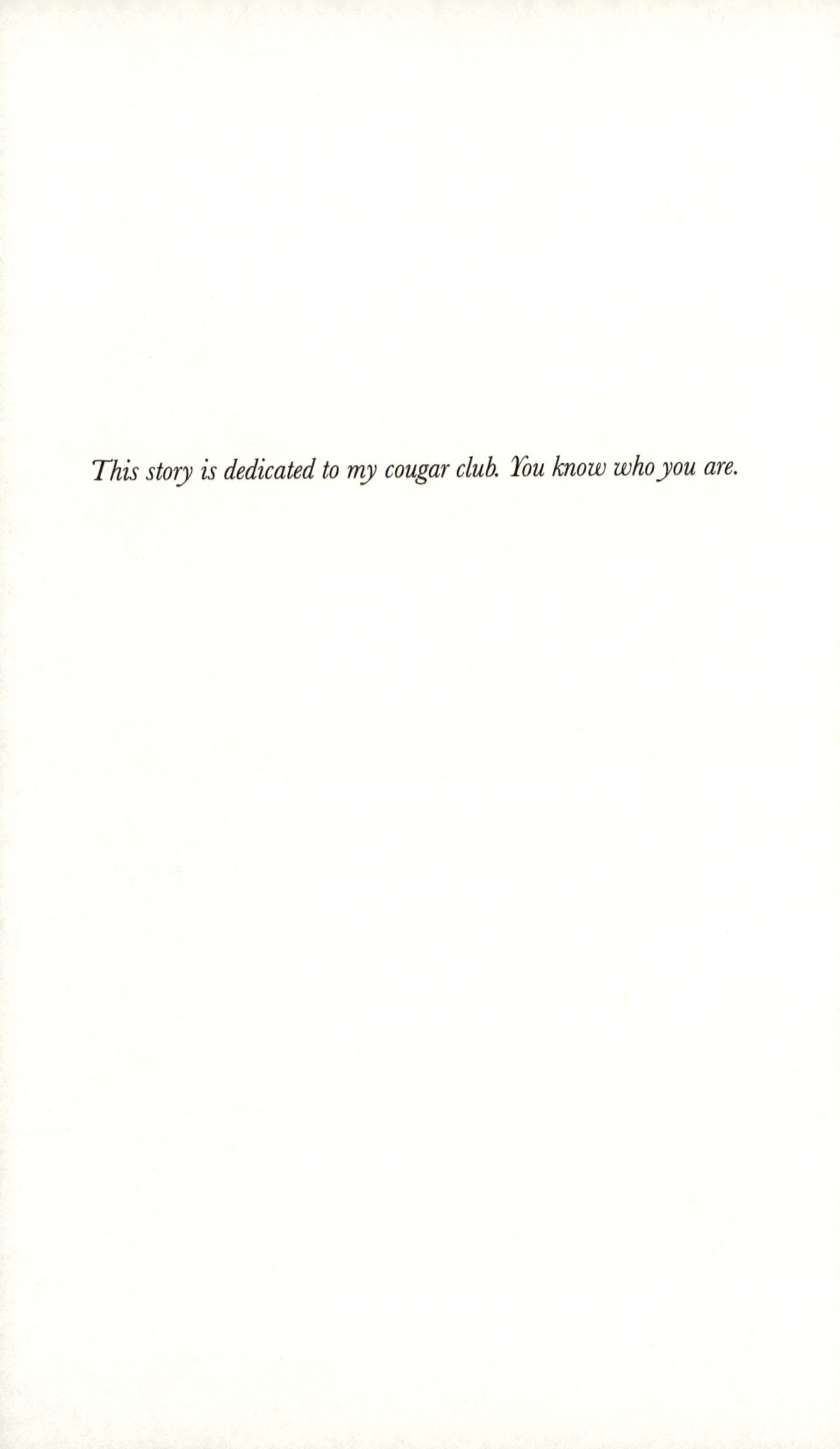

This story is dedicated to my cougar club. You know who you are.

PRAISE FOR SATURDAY NIGHT SPECIAL

"5 HUGE STARS!!" ★★★★★ *Karla, Goodreads*

"Not only is it **VERY** funny, it's also full of plot with some crazy supporting characters." ★★★★★ *Kimber with Guilty Pleasures Book Review, Goodreads*

"By far the **best** and **funniest** of the series." ★★★★★ *Cindy, Goodreads*

"I know I have the 7th and final book to read in the series, but I'm going to ahead and say **there's no way Ms. Carr can top this one**." ★★★★★ *Kim O, Goodreads*

"What can I say this book was **hysterical** and **hot**!" ★★★★★ *Maureen Ames, Goodreads*

"I **giggled**, I **chuckled** and I **guffawed**." ★★★★★ *Melanie Marnell, Goodreads*

"I **laughed** and I **cried** the whole way through this book." ★★★★★ *Katherine, Goodreads*

"All I can say if you don't read this book **you are missing something really special**." ★★★★★ *John, Goodreads*

"Carr's writing is **fast-paced and full of wit**." ★★★★★ *LynnMarie, Goodreads*

"OMG! This book is DEFINETELY on my top 3 MOST FUNNIEST BOOKS READ THIS YEAR! I still can't stop **LAUGHING**! People at the office were like...."ok, what's so funny?" **RILEY COLLINS**! THAT'S WHAT'S FUNNY!" ★★★★★ *Sophie with Book Suburbia, Goodreads*

"Well if I could **give more stars I would**." ★★★★★ *Toni Lewis, Goodreads*

"This series just gets **better** and **better** with each book." ★★★★★ *Sarah, Goodreads*

"An entertaining steamy short story with lots of **zany characters**." ★★★★★ *Dawn, Goodreads*

"What a **hoot**!! A laugh out loud, **smex-a-poolza** should be the tag line for this book." ★ ★ ★ ★ ★ *Dar, Goodreads*

PLAYLIST

Fans of Spotify! Now you can access the Wild Irish "titles" playlist.

Come Monday – Jimmy Buffett
Ruby Tuesday – The Rolling Stones.
Waiting for Wednesday – Lisa Loeb and Nine Stories.
Sweet Thursday – Matt Costa
Friday I'm in Love – The Cure
Saturday Night Special – Lynard Skynard
Any Given Sunday – Sandpeople

MONDAY'S CHILD

Monday's child is fair of face,
Tuesday's child is full of grace,
Wednesday's child is full of woe,
Thursday's child has far to go,
Friday's child is loving and giving,
Saturday's child works hard for a living,
But the child who is born on the Sabbath day,
Is bonny and blithe and good and gay.

~ Traditional nursery rhyme

CHAPTER ONE

Aaron Young walked into the Mirage and took a deep breath, trying to calm his ragged nerves. After all, Riley had called her sister Keira and told her where she was, and that she was fine. Unfortunately, that wasn't registering in his incensed mind. She'd run off to Las Vegas with Trevor Blankenship, the biggest moron in their graduating class, on a drunken whim. The fact that Trevor was newly separated from his wife wasn't helping to calm Aaron. The asshole wasn't even pursuing a divorce, if the local gossip was accurate.

What the hell was she thinking?

Aaron walked through the miles and miles of gambling tables and slot machines, well aware that finding Riley in the massive casino was a bit like trying to find an honest politician in D.C. For a second, he wondered if he should have left a trail of breadcrumbs or something. He was afraid he'd get lost forever in this maze of mind-numbing noise and flashing lights.

A loud cheer captured his attention and he spotted a large crowd. Bingo. He headed toward the gathering, unsurprised when he saw Riley's bouncing brunette curls at the center of the group. The lively woman always managed to attract the loudest, rowdiest sort of people, regardless of the setting.

She laughed and did some sort of victory dance with the woman next to her that reminded him of Beyonce's *Single Ladies* video. He grinned despite his anger. Damn, she knew how to have fun. It had always been this way.

He'd met Riley Collins when they were both three years old and their mothers struck up a conversation at the playground. From that day 'til now, he and Riley had been best friends, in an "opposites attract" sort of way. While Riley was the life of every party, Aaron was more content to hover in the background. Happy to watch her shine. She was beautiful and dynamic, perfect in every way.

Except when she pulled stunts like this little impromptu excursion to Vegas. Then she frustrated the hell out of him, drove him insane. Sadly, her wild escapades had become more frequent and more dangerous since the wedding of her older sister Teagan. She was headed for disaster, and for some reason, her brothers and pop were looking to Aaron to rein her in. He snorted. None of the males in the Collins family had managed to control Riley the past twenty-five years, so he wasn't sure what magic they expected *him* to work.

Keira had called him, frantic, when she'd learned

Riley—after a long night of partying—had hopped on a red-eye flight to Vegas. Now here he stood, early Saturday evening, watching the source of his annoyance putting another twenty dollar bet on the blackjack table. Standing behind her, a totally wasted Trevor had his hand down the front of a bleached-blonde woman's sequin dress.

This day kept getting better and better.

The dealer placed more winnings in front of Riley and Aaron decided now might be a good time to break up the party. Find a way to convince her to quit while she was ahead.

He shoved his way through the rambunctious crowd, his police training and large build coming in handy. A few people looked as if they wanted to protest the fact he was pushing them aside, but backed off when they saw his determined face. He intended to get Riley Collins' perky little ass out of this casino and on the next plane back to Baltimore— and he didn't care who he had hurt to make that happen.

He squeezed in between Riley and the woman next to her. The dealer looked up, perhaps ready to tell him the table was full, but he closed his mouth when Aaron flashed him an angry look.

Riley grinned when she spotted him, the only person he'd encountered thus far who didn't seem confused or annoyed by his pushy arrival.

"Hey, sugar," she slurred. Great, she was drunk. That helped him ignore the pleasure that suffused his body when she called him by her nickname for him.

"What the fuck are you doing here, Riley?" His voice was deep and clearly furious.

She shrugged, oblivious to his feelings. "Playing blackjack." Then she really looked at him and started to giggle. "Oh my God, Aaron. Did you know you're in Vegas?"

"Yeah, I had a few clues, but I think it was the seven-hour flight and hour layover in Chicago that sort of solidified it for me."

Riley laughed, dismissing his angry sarcasm as humor. "Hey, Trev." She turned to get the attention of the man Aaron was three seconds away from laying out on the floor with his fist. "Look who's here. My BFF Aaron."

Trevor looked up, his surprise muted by his downright drunkenness. "Hey, Aaron." Trevor's arm was still slung around a woman Aaron would bet his entire retirement fund was a prostitute.

"Trevor," he forced out in as calm a fashion as he could manage.

Trevor stepped over to him and slapped him on the shoulder, staggering a bit as he walked. "I'm glad you're here, man. Me and Bella were just going up to my room. Maybe you wouldn't mind keeping an eye on ol' Riley for me." The drunken ass followed up his comment with a lecherous wink, as if Aaron couldn't figure out what he intended to do with the woman in the hotel room.

Aaron narrowed his eyes furiously, perfectly aware Trevor would have left Riley alone regardless of his arrival. He consciously took a deep breath and nodded.

"You have money, Trev?" He hated that for some reason he felt the need to protect the dumbass. Unfortunately, the last thing he needed to deal with was Trevor stiffing a hooker—literally and figuratively. He was pretty sure the high-school quarterback, who also had the distinct honor of having the lowest GPA in their graduating class, had no idea his "date" for the evening would expect to be paid for her efforts.

Sure enough, Trevor's forehead creased in confusion. "Um, yeah. Why? You need a few bucks for the slots?"

"No," he said, "just making sure you didn't need any."

Trevor smiled at what he no doubt thought was a generous offer. "Ah no, man. I'm good. Thanks, though. I'll catch you later, Riley."

"Okie-dokie, Trev. See you later." Riley grabbed her poker chips and headed toward the slot machines. Trevor pinched the blonde woman's ass and she laughed, taking his hand and leading him to a bank of elevators.

"Nice of you to keep me company. Trevor was starting to get on my nerves. Jesus, he's thick," Riley said as he followed her to a Lucky Seven Bars machine. She almost fell in her attempt to sit down and he steadied her with a firm hand on her back. Shit, how much had she had to drink?

"You've known Trevor for years, Riley. What made you think he'd be an entertaining traveling companion?" He claimed the stool next to hers.

"I don't know. I just wanted to do something fun

and he was sulking over Johanna kicking him out, so we decided to get out of town for a while."

"Why didn't you call me?" He was hurt she'd chosen to take off with Trevor rather than him.

"Yeah right," she said with a laugh. "I'm *so* sure you would have hopped on a plane to Vegas with me. You would have had seven hundred and ninety-eight reasons why we couldn't come here. Trevor just said sure."

He considered her words. She was right. He would have tried to talk her out of it. Hell, he probably would have succeeded. "But Trevor?"

"He's harmless as a puppy and you know it. You didn't think I'd run away with him romantically, did you?" She laughed hysterically when his face betrayed that thought had briefly crossed his mind.

"Holy shit," she said once she'd regained control. She waved a waitress over and helped herself to one of the free drinks on the woman's tray. "That is just freaking twisted, sugar."

He sighed heavily. One question was tormenting him. "What are you doing in Vegas, Riley?"

"Gambling."

"Very funny." He grimaced, not amused by her joke.

"I'm having fun, Aaron. You know, that thing you've never quite mastered?"

He sucked in a deep breath and counted to ten. Riley constantly teased him about being a stick in the mud. He knew it was said in good fun, but this time her words felt more like an insult than a joke. Sometimes it sucked being regarded as the boring, responsible one among their group of friends.

Need a ride home from the bar? Call Aaron. Got a flat tire? Aaron will have a jack…and a spare. Moving? Aaron will lug all your shit down three flights of stairs *and* supply the truck to haul it.

A growl rose up in his chest. He was pissed off at Riley for thinking him so dull he wouldn't do anything as spontaneous as taking a weekend trip to Vegas.

"You seriously call hopping on a plane and flying to Vegas with Trevor Blankenship 'fun'? I call it fucking dangerous."

"Bullshit. I haven't done anything even remotely dangerous…yet. I called Keira and told her where I was and I didn't come alone. I came with a friend." Riley threw another dollar in the machine.

"You didn't call Keira until after you were already here."

"And like the good sister she is, she called you to come save the day. Right?"

"She was worried about you, Riley."

"I'm a big girl, sugar. A fact my family and you seem content to ignore."

"I'm not forgetting you're an adult. I'm just not overlooking the fact you're completely drunk in a strange town with Trevor and a hooker as your chaperones."

Riley's gaze traveled from the slot machine to Aaron. "I told Trev she was a hooker, but he wouldn't believe me." She took a long drink before setting the cup down and hitting the Spin button again.

"What are you drinking?" He picked up her glass and drained it. Alcohol suddenly seemed like a very good idea. He waved over the waitress and grabbed his own drink.

"Tasted like something with rum to me," she said. "You better take it easy on that. I'm already wasted. If you keep pounding those down, who'll get us home?"

He shrugged and took another swig. Now that he was here, he wasn't in any big hurry to leave. "It takes a lot to get me drunk."

"Yeah, well, maybe you should consider taking up the hobby. Drunk seems to be the best way to live in dreary Baltimore nowadays." Her tone was sullen, belligerent, and he wondered at her words.

"Since when is Baltimore dreary? You love the city."

She sobered up a bit and he was struck by the hint of sadness in her eyes. When he thought back on it, he realized the same look had been there often the past few months. Why hadn't he noticed it sooner?

"So I guess now I *don't* love the city. Dammit, I just can't do it anymore, Aaron."

"Do what?"

"My life. I can't wake up in the same bedroom I've lived in since birth one more morning. I can't cook meals in that damn pub day in and day out anymore and I'm sick to death of partying with the same losers every Saturday night."

Her voice was filled with resentment, frustration, and he listened as the last detail—and he suspected the most important one—fell from her lips.

"I'm the last Collins kid at home. I'm it. The spinster sister," she added.

He burst into laughter. He knew she was being serious, but her words were so insanely funny he couldn't hold back his instinctive response.

Her eyes narrowed angrily. "What's so funny?"

"You," he said with a chuckle, "calling yourself a spinster. Two things I never thought I'd hear together in the same sentence. Riley Collins, the spinster." Repeating the words caused him to laugh again and some of the irritation he'd been harboring since leaving BWI that morning dissipated. Actually, simply finding her safe and sound had dispelled most of it.

"It's not funny. I've watched both my sisters find true love. They're living their happily ever afters while I'm still stuck at home alone with Pop."

"Happily ever afters? True love?" Aaron repeated. "Sounds pretty romantic for you, Riley. How much have you had to drink?"

"Ha ha. I've had too much and I'm gonna have more, but it doesn't matter. I'll still be fed up and lonely tomorrow."

Aaron looked at her dark brown eyes and felt a hope he'd never experienced stir inside him. "You said you never wanted to get married. You said it would cut in to your fun time, your independence. You've sworn off the entire institution since we were three."

"Yeah," she said. "Well, I changed my mind."

Aaron considered her words for a moment, and then gave in to the grin building in his chest. "Good."

"Good?"

He nodded, grasping her by the waist to set her on her feet. "Very good. Come on."

He took her hand and pulled her toward the foyer of the casino. She didn't fight him and instead followed easily, if somewhat unsteadily.

"Where are we going?" she asked as they stopped for a moment while Aaron got his bearings. It was early evening, but given the crowds in front of the hotel, it was clear Las Vegas was just getting started.

"You'll see."

"So long as you aren't taking me home," she said. "I don't wanna go home yet."

"You aren't going home."

"I don't wanna go to the room either."

"You aren't."

She giggled, muttering something about not believing he'd chased her all the way to Vegas.

Obviously she was more than tipsy. He grinned. Tipsy was just the way he wanted her for once. He pulled a map of the Las Vegas strip he'd bought at the airport out of his pocket and consulted it. When he found what he was looking for, he put his arm around her shoulders and urged her toward the taxi stand, where they were promptly ushered into a waiting vehicle.

"Aaron, where are we going?"

"You'll see," he repeated, giving the driver the address and fighting to ignore the grin that crossed the older man's face as he glanced at Riley.

"Good for you," the man said, turning and pulling on to the street. As the taxi driver fought the

Saturday evening traffic, Aaron took in the sights of the strip, overwhelmed and amazed by the bright lights. Vegas was quite a city and he was suddenly thankful he'd come. This was going to be a weekend to remember.

The driver pulled up in front of their destination. Aaron paid the driver before bending to help Riley out of the cab.

"Courthouse?" She glanced up at the nondescript building.

"We'll need a marriage license before we hit the Elvis Wedding Chapel."

"Elvis Wedding Chapel? What the hell are you talking about?" She stared at him and for a moment he thought she would balk at his suggestion, refuse him and storm away.

"We're getting hitched."

Riley laughed. "You and me?"

"Why not? We'll just call it the ultimate Saturday Night Special."

She paused for a moment, the alcohol fogging her mind nicely. She considered his proposal before shrugging playfully. Riley was the queen of Saturday Night Specials, the name she'd given to her evening off from work. It was the one night of the week when she usually got into a lot of trouble that he inevitably had to get her out of.

"Why not? We *are* in Vegas. Okay, come on! This story will be funny as shit when I tell everyone at home. Riley's Saturday Night Special, Vegas-style!"

Riley was a born storyteller, one of the reasons he

suspected she always attracted a crowd. She was entertaining and her stories were hilarious.

They bought the license, traveled to the chapel and said their "I dos" under the watchful eye of the Asian Elvis who married them. He serenaded them back out onto the street as Mr. and Mrs. Aaron Young to the tune of *Love Me Tender* while Riley giggled.

They returned to the hotel and scored a table at Fin, one of the Mirage's trendy restaurants, despite their lack of reservations. While there, they consumed two bottles of champagne, toasting their long lives together and stuffing themselves on Chinese cuisine.

Finally, Aaron suggested they start the honeymoon. They staggered to Riley's room, laughing the entire way, and he carried her over the threshold as Riley squealed with delight.

As he carried her to the bed, he was struck by the memory of carrying her to her bed the night of Teagan's wedding. She'd had too much champagne that night too.

"You're crazy," she said with a giggle. "I can't believe we just got married. Do you know what a pain in the ass this will be to untangle tomorrow when we're sober?"

"It'll work out." He placed her on her feet by the bed, gripping her shoulders to keep her steady. She reached up and he was stunned to feel her fingers unbuttoning his shirt. While he wasn't completely drunk, he couldn't say he wasn't enjoying the effects of the alcohol. A quick glance at Riley's face confirmed she was extremely intoxicated. He stilled her hands as she reached for the last button.

"I can do that," he said. "Let me help you." He pulled her sweater over her head. Modesty had never been an issue for Riley. She didn't possess any and she laughed again.

"What's so funny?" he asked.

"How many times have you tucked me in?"

"A million," he answered seriously.

"Yeah, a million."

He helped her pull her jeans down. He'd seen her in her bra and panties many, many times before but this time it was different. *She* may not know it, but *he* did.

He drew back the sheets and she climbed in. This time, unlike the million times in the past, he didn't leave. He tugged off his shirt and pants and crawled in beside her. His actions sent her into peals of laughter again.

"This is weird."

"Not really." He pressed a light kiss on her forehead. "Good night, Mrs. Young."

She grinned, her eyes drooping. The alcohol was claiming her quickly. "Kiss me good night."

"I just did."

"No, really kiss me. You never have."

She was right. A lifetime of friendship and he'd never kissed Riley Collins. He'd dreamed of it since puberty, but he'd never done it.

He leaned forward and brushed her lips lightly with his. It was enough for now. When he kissed her for real, she'd be sober, awake and aware.

She was asleep before he moved away and he grinned. The woman could fall asleep within seconds of putting her head on a pillow.

"Good night, wife," he whispered, wrapping his arm around her and pulling her close.

CHAPTER TWO

"What the fuck?" Riley woke up disoriented and thirsty, and her head was pounding. All of that was pretty common for a Sunday morning. What was *not* common was a nearly naked Aaron spooning her in bed.

"Good morning, Riley," he said, as if he didn't have a concern in the world. As if there was no reason she should be freaking out. She wiggled a little, hoping to break free of his embrace, but stopped immediately when something hard brushed against her ass.

"What is that?" she asked when he chuckled. It was obvious he didn't give a shit his cock was fully erect and nudging her lower regions through the thin cotton layer provided by his boxers.

"Somebody else's way of saying good morning."

She lifted the sheets an inch or two and glanced down, only mildly relieved to discover she was in her bra and panties. If they'd fooled around, she would have been naked, right? He wouldn't have his boxers on. *Right? Holy shit, please let that be right.*

He pulled her back closer to his bare chest and she stiffened at the idea of being cuddled, in bed, by Aaron. That they'd hugged thousands of times in the past twenty years was inconsequential, especially considering that during those platonic embraces they'd always been dressed…and standing up.

"This is Las Vegas," she mumbled, glancing around the hotel room.

"It sure is."

"I thought I came to Vegas with Trevor." She closed her eyes and tried to force her mushy brain to remember the previous evening. Hell, she'd be happy to remember the night *before* last.

That's it. I'm never drinking again.

"You did come with Trev. I followed you." Aaron's grip on her waist tightened briefly before his hand moved, his fingers roaming suggestively on her stomach.

Oh shit. Aaron stroking her skin should not feel so good. Had he always been this muscular? This built? This sexy? His typically short black hair had gotten longer in the last few months, and she wondered what it would feel like to run her fingers through it. She was suddenly having very impure thoughts about her best friend. She forced herself to ignore his touches as she tried to remember what he'd said.

"Why did you follow me?"

"I was worried about you, Riley. You took off with

Trevor. He's not exactly known for his intellect or sobriety."

"Where *is* Trev?" She prayed he wasn't in the room as well.

"Last time I saw him, he was heading for a hotel room with some hooker named Bella."

"Riiiiight." She dragged out the word, trying to recall if she'd actually met this Bella chick.

"You don't remember that?" His hand paused an inch above her panty line and she was two seconds away from suggesting he move it just a bit farther south. She loved morning sex.

Fuck! This is Aaron. Stop it, Riley.

"I don't remember the hooker," she admitted.

"What do you remember?"

She took a deep breath and forced herself to roll to her back. She needed to see his face, wanted to read his expressions in some vain hope of figuring out what the hell was going on. He allowed her to turn but his hand never left her body. She tried to calm her racing heart at the feeling of his palm resting against her bare skin.

"I remember landing in Vegas and hitting the strip. There were these blue drinks at a bar. After that, it gets kinda hazy."

"Blue drinks?" he asked, his chocolate-brown eyes narrowing thoughtfully.

"You weren't there for those?"

He shook his head, unconcerned. "I must have missed the blue drinks. I made it in time for the good stuff though."

His sleep-tousled hair sent her body into overdrive,

as did his husky morning voice. Christ, she was totally attracted to him.

To Aaron.

Maybe she was still drunk and the alcohol was affecting her brain. His hand started to caress her stomach again and she brought hers down quickly to halt his movements.

Time to bite the bullet. Ask the most important question.

"Why are you in bed with me?"

Aaron grinned. "Where else would I be?"

"Ordinarily I would say at home, cussing me and my wild schemes. But at the very least, given that we're not in Baltimore, you should be in your *own* hotel room."

He chuckled. "Well, I guess I don't have to worry about your wild schemes anymore—or the separate hotel rooms."

"Why is that?" A strong sense of impending trouble suffused her as she asked the question. Some part of her knew instinctively she didn't want to hear the answer.

He lifted her left hand up with his and pointed to a thick silver band on her ring finger.

"What the fuck is *that*?"

"Your wedding ring. We're married."

"The hell we are!"

He shrugged off her heated denial with a good-natured smile and her arousal vanished in an instant, replaced by the need to hit something or someone. She narrowed her eyes, wondering what it would feel like to punch him in the stomach. No doubt that would shrink Mr. Happy back to a manageable size. As it was, she was finding it very difficult to think with his cock poking her in the hip with every breath she took.

"Can't you put that thing away?" she yelled, pointing at his hard-on.

"Away…or in?"

She gasped at the thought. "I have to get out of here." She started to rise but Aaron quite efficiently managed to stop her, moving over her and pinning her to the bed with his hips and hands. She was completely trapped, surrounded by his hard flesh.

"No more running away, Riley."

She placed her palms against his chest, intending to shove him off, but his words halted her actions. "What's that supposed to mean? I don't run away."

"All you do is run. You aren't going to escape this so easily."

She tried to assimilate this man, this Aaron, with the man who'd been her gentle best friend for over two decades. "Escape what?"

"Our marriage." He punctuated his words with a slow, firm thrust of his erection against the vee of her legs.

"We aren't married."

He grinned. "We are very, very married. I have the marriage license and the DVD to prove it."

"DVD?"

"I figured some of the details might be hazy for you. Besides, it's a nice keepsake. Something we can show our kids."

"Okay, that's it." She pushed against his chest, desperate to break free of his overwhelming presence. She'd never felt so thoroughly surrounded. "You're going to have to shut the hell up. If we *did* get married, I was drunk and it was a mistake. One we can take care of if you would just let me up." When he failed to budge, her shoves turned to slaps. "Get off me!"

He shook his head and lowered until he was supporting his upper body with his elbows, rather than his hands. His chest crushed her breasts and his lips were less than an inch from hers. She felt a slight tremor rumble through her. She wanted to believe it was based on fear, but she was pretty sure it had everything in the world to do with arousal. He was pushing all her hot buttons with this caveman posturing.

Aaron had never taken charge of any aspect of their friendship, content to let her lead the way in all things. Feeling his power over her sent a rush of heat to every part of her body.

His eyes narrowed angrily and she felt a strange sense of pleasure at having knocked some of the damn annoying happiness out of him. "Our marriage was not a mistake and I don't ever want to hear you say that again."

She closed her eyes, his breath hot on her cheek. It was taking every ounce of strength in her body not to move her lips the little baby inch it would take to touch his. "Please be reasonable," she said. "This can't work."

"Why not?"

She sighed. "We're too different."

"That hasn't stopped us from being friends—best friends—for over twenty years."

"There's a helluva lot more to marriage than just friendship, sugar." The moment the words crossed her lips, she knew she'd made a mistake.

"That's right. There is." He pressed his cock against her suddenly damp panties again. Jesus, she wished he'd stop doing that. It was all she could do not to invite him in and damn the cost.

"You know, you're coming very close to losing that thing." She wished the threat didn't sound so weak.

"I wouldn't mind losing it for a while—inside you."

"Ugh."

He laughed at her feigned disgust. "Last night you begged me to kiss you good night."

"I was drunk."

He moved forward slowly until their noses nearly touched. "Don't you want to know about the kiss?"

"No, and you shouldn't be bragging about taking advantage of an intoxicated woman. If my brothers were here, they'd kick your ass."

"I don't think there's anything wrong with kissing a woman if she's your wife and it's your honeymoon."

"Oh shit. We had sex, didn't we?" She racked her brain, trying to recall some small part of the previous night. How could she sleep with her best friend and not remember it?

Aaron started to move his hips, rubbing his cock suggestively against her covered pussy. She fought to ignore how good it felt. He leaned closer, his breath scorching her cheek as his lips moved toward her ear. "No," he whispered. "We didn't have sex."

Relief claimed her, but it was short-lived when his fingers twined in her hair and he directed her face toward his.

"And I still owe you the kiss," he murmured a moment before his lips claimed hers.

Christ, claimed was right. Riley had never been kissed so passionately in her life. Aaron's mouth moved over hers, demanding, taking, possessing. He pushed her lips apart, his tongue plunging into her mouth to explore. His fingers tightened around her curls, controlling her movements, putting her where he wanted her. Her brain wanted to resist but it was powerless to control her hyper-aroused body. The kiss seemed to last for hours and for a moment, Riley considered the fact she'd wasted years of her life kissing assholes while this champion kisser was standing next to her all along.

When Aaron finally pulled back, she was surprised to discover her hands were wrapped around his neck, holding him to her.

"Fuck." She'd never felt so confused; so conflicted and torn. This was Aaron. This was wrong.

"Okay," he said, and she laughed. She couldn't help it. His goofy, good-natured attitude always managed to cheer her up.

"You're incorrigible."

"Does that mean we can have sex?" he asked.

"Can we wait until my hangover goes away? I really can't think straight right now."

He nodded, placing a quick kiss on the end of her

nose. He moved back to her side, pulling her until her head rested on his bare chest. She wasn't used to him being so controlling. She wished it wasn't turning her on so much.

"Maybe we should get up," she suggested, even though she didn't move. Her head hurt too badly. Besides, she was comfy and warm.

"Not yet," he said. "Just rest awhile."

They lay in companionable silence for several minutes and Riley had just about let the slow pounding of his heart lure her back to sleep when there was a knock at the door.

"Ignore it," she said sleepily. "Maybe they'll go away."

Aaron gently moved her aside and stood up. "I don't think you want me to ignore *this* visitor."

"Aaron, I'm half naked and hung over. Believe me, there is no one I want to see." She pulled the covers over her head as he yanked on his jeans and walked to the door.

She listened from under the blanket as he spoke to someone. She couldn't make out what was said, but she heard Aaron say thanks and shut the door again. She lowered the covers a little bit to peer out, surprised to find him holding a McDonald's bag for her to see.

She sat up quickly, grabbing her head as her too-fast movement sent a sharp pain through her temple. "Ouch. Damn head. Is that what I think it is?"

"If you think it's one Riley Collins Hangover Cure, then yep, it's what you think."

"How the hell did you get McDonald's delivered through room service?"

"It's Vegas. You can get anything if you're willing to pay. I bribed one of the bellhops last night when we got in. Promised him a big tip if he would pick it up and deliver it."

He handed her the bag and she pulled out the still-warm hash brown, holding it as if it were a precious treasure. "Manna from heaven."

"Aren't you forgetting something?"

She looked up, delighted when he pulled a drink from behind his back.

"Diet Coke?" she asked.

"Would I get you anything else?"

"Oh, Aaron, you are too good to me."

He laughed. "You're an easy woman to please. Couple of hash browns and a soda."

"No better food on earth the day after a long party. I can't believe you went to so much trouble."

"You're worth it."

She took the drink from him and looked away quickly, afraid to let him see how much his words were affecting her. He said nice things to her all the time. Aaron always did sweet, thoughtful things. Now, however, his actions seemed more apparent, more important. She had no doubt he meant for them to stay married. The thought he wanted such a thing blew her away. He'd never come on to her, never flirted with her, never made her believe they'd ever be anything more than friends. Overnight, somehow, all that had changed and she couldn't figure out how to feel about it.

"Are you going to eat that or try to stare it into your stomach?"

"Why do you want to be married to me?" she asked.

If Aaron was taken aback by her question, it didn't show. He sat beside her on the bed and shrugged. "There are a lot of reasons why, Riley."

"Name a few."

"We're compatible. We have fun together. You're damn easy on the eyes."

She snorted. "You think I'm pretty?"

"Hell yeah. I think you're gorgeous."

"Since when?" she asked with a laugh. "In middle school, you called me Metal Mouth."

"You had braces. Besides, that was years ago. You can't hold me accountable for mean nicknames I used when I was eleven. If I recall correctly, you called me Aaron Dung."

"Oh my God. I forgot about that. You gotta admit that was a pretty good one, Young."

"Yeah well, we'll call that argument a draw." He reached over and ran his finger down her cheek and she could see in his eyes he meant what he said about finding her attractive.

"Liking someone's looks isn't a real solid basis for a marriage, sugar."

"I wasn't finished giving you my reasons. You can cook. You're smart. You'll make one helluva good mother and I want to fuck you so bad it hurts."

Riley opened her mouth to respond, but no words would come.

"Left you speechless, eh?" he asked. "Never thought I'd see the day."

"You can't be serious," she said when she finally found her voice.

"My cock's been knocking on those lace panties all morning, Riley." As he spoke he pointed at his erection, clearly visible through the denim of his jeans. "What did you interpret that as? Mild interest?"

"Guys always wake up with hard-ons. I just thought it was testosterone."

Aaron rolled his eyes. "If that were the case it would have deflated after a few minutes. I'm feeling lightheaded from the fact all the blood in my body has been hanging out south of the border for nearly an hour."

"Sounds painful."

He wiggled his eyebrows. "Wanna kiss it better?"

She was saved from answering when someone else knocked on the door. "More hash browns?"

He shook his head. "Nope. Probably the maid." He rose and opened the door. Riley only had a moment to pull the covers up before Johanna Blankenship, Trev's estranged wife, came running into the room with a baseball bat.

"Son of a bitch!" she yelled as she stormed straight toward the bed. "Where is he? The cheating bastard! Fucking man whore! I'm gonna bash his brains in!"

"Whoa, Jo. Take it easy," Aaron said, and she turned, swinging the bat. He dodged out of the way, escaping a nasty hit by inches.

"Oh. Sorry, Aaron. I thought you were Trev."

"Jesus, Johanna. Put the bat down," Riley said. "You're gonna hurt somebody with that thing."

Johanna spun, her fury finding a new victim as she approached the bed. "Don't you lecture me, you filthy home wrecker." Jo raised the bat but before she could bring it down, Aaron grabbed the weapon and the woman from behind.

Riley felt her temper snap at the woman's near assault and dropped the sheet, rising up on her knees, despite the fact she was only in her bra and panties. "Home wrecker? Are you kidding me? You seriously think I'd want that dumbass husband of yours?"

"Riley." Aaron struggled to hold on to Johanna, who was screeching obscenities and struggling to get free. "Maybe now's not a good time to throw around insults."

"Dumbass? How dare you call my husband stupid!"

"Well, *you* just called him a man whore," Riley retorted.

"I can call him anything I want. He's *my* husband—and you ran off to Vegas with him, knowing full well he has a wife at home! Bet you didn't count on your sister telling me where to find you!"

Riley made a mental note to kill Keira later. "Oh for pity's sake, I did not *run off* with Trev."

"Then why are you nearly naked in that bed?" Johanna asked, while Aaron retained his death grip on her arm and the bat.

"Because I was *asleep*. Besides, if you look around, I think you'll notice your husband isn't in this room."

Riley's comment seemed to penetrate and the wind

left Johanna's sails. Jo turned around and Riley fought back a groan as Trev's gossip-loving wife took in Aaron's state of undress before turning back to study her again with a smirk.

"Don't look at me like that, Johanna," she warned. "It's not what you think."

"Of course it is," Aaron interjected. "Riley and I eloped last night. You actually caught us in the middle of our honeymoon, so if you don't mind—"

Aaron's comments, rather than sparking Johanna's nosy interest, released an onslaught of loud sobs. For several moments, he stood speechless as Johanna bawled inconsolably.

"What did I say?" he asked Riley.

"This is not helping my headache," Riley replied.

"Could you try to have a little compassion?" Aaron wrapped an arm around Johanna's shoulder.

Riley rolled her eyes in response but the gesture sent another stab of pain through her temple. Johanna had tried to take her head off with a baseball bat and insulted her intelligence. Aaron could be compassionate if he wanted, but Riley was feeling a bit low on that emotion.

"Me and Trev eloped t-too," Johanna stammered, the words hard to understand through her crying. "We drove over to Paw Paw, West Virginia, where his uncle was the justice of the peace, and then we went to his family's hunting cabin for our honeymoon. It was deer season and he gave me a new rifle as a wedding gift."

"Romantic," Riley muttered, but she shut up when

Aaron sent her a dirty look. He led Jo to the single chair in the room.

If there was one thing Aaron was a sucker for, it was tears. Riley had teased him mercilessly over the years for what she called his Achilles heel. If a woman wanted to get his attention, she merely had to pour on the waterworks. He had dated crazy Louise Perkins for six months longer than he'd wanted to during his junior year in high school, simply because she cried every time he suggested they break up. Riley had finally intervened, convincing Louise she'd be much happier dating Chuckie Haines.

"Please don't get so upset, Johanna. I'm sure Trevor's just blowing off some steam. He knows he's got a good thing at home with you. He's not going to mess that up," Aaron said.

"I'm sorry," she said between sniffles. "It's all these damn hormones. I c-cry at the drop of a hat nowadays."

"Hormones?" Riley asked.

"I found out I'm pregnant a couple days ago. I went to find Trev to tell him he was gonna be a daddy, but then I heard the two of you had run off to Vegas."

"Pregnant. Wow. Congratulations, Jo," Riley said. *Jesus, Trevor has reproduced.*

"So if you and Trev didn't run off together, where is he?" Johanna asked. "I want to tell him the good news."

Riley glanced at Aaron, who shrugged. She recalled him telling her about Trev hooking up with a prostitute. "He, um, he just stepped out for some breakfast," she lied, rising from the bed and edging her way toward the bathroom. If things turned nasty again, Riley was fully prepared to hunker down behind a locked door. Besides, she had to pee.

"Where?" Jo asked.

"I'm not sure where he was headed. Just called a few minutes ago and said he was going to get something to eat." While Riley was disgusted with Trev for cheating on his wife, she couldn't completely hang the man out to dry. She'd spent at least an hour of Friday night listening to him cry in his beer over missing Jo. Regardless of his infidelity, he loved his wife and she figured he deserved a chance to make amends if he wanted to. After all, he was going to be a father.

"Tell you what, Johanna. Why don't you see if you can get a room here at the hotel and Riley and I will go find him?" Aaron suggested.

"We will?" Riley asked.

"Yes, we will. You're probably tired after the flight and that's not good for you or the baby. Call us with your room number, take a nice long bath and we'll send Trevor to your room when we find him. In fact, you can surprise him. The two of you can have a romantic night together and celebrate. How does that sound?"

Johanna smiled at him as she stood. "That's a great idea. My feet are killing me. Thank you, Aaron. And congratulations on your marriage." She started to walk out of the room but turned at the last minute to look at Riley. "Bye, Riley. No hard feelings?"

"We're good, Jo." Riley waved and watched the woman retrieve her luggage from where she'd left it in the hall. Aaron closed the door and leaned on it wearily.

"You forgot to give her back her bat. She may want that when she finds out what Trev's been up to," she said.

"That's exactly why I kept it."

"So, Mr. Wonderful, any ideas on where we're supposed to find Trevor and the hooker? Vegas is kind of a big place, you know."

"I'll call the front desk and see if he's still here."

"Don't you think Johanna asked about Trev first? He's probably checked out."

"I'm still calling the clerk. Who knows what Johanna asked and it's worth a try."

Riley dressed while Aaron placed the call. She listened as he questioned the clerk and she could tell from the conversation he wasn't having much luck getting any answers. She didn't expect he would, but her cop was clearly on the case.

"Well?" she asked when he hung up.

"All he would tell me is that Trev checked out last night. Probably broke a rule telling me that much, but I mentioned the worried, pregnant wife."

"Wonder if he was still with Bella when he left."

"I suppose we could try to track down the clerk on duty last night, see if he remembers anything Trev said when he checked out. If Bella was still with him, I sort of think the clerk would remember."

"Why's that?" she asked.

"Bella makes quite an impression. She's sort of..." Aaron gestured with his hands in front of his chest.

"Stacked?" Riley asked and he nodded.

"Oh hell yeah," he said, so reverently she rolled her eyes.

"What is it with guys and big boobs? They're just fat and skin."

Aaron shrugged. "They're fun to play with."

"Let's roll. The sooner we find Trev, the sooner we can straighten out this marriage mess we're in. And for the record, I don't appreciate you telling Jo we're married. You know what a gossip she is. She's probably already called half of Baltimore with the news. My family will freak."

"We *are* married, Riley, and the only problem we need to correct is the lack of honeymoon boom-boom."

"Oh, that's very funny. What are you, three years old?"

As she reached to open the door, she was surprised when Aaron turned her and pushed her against it forcefully. He pressed his body against hers and in an instant she felt the arousal she'd only just managed to beat down come surging to the surface again. It seemed that with one firm touch or heated look, he could drive her to the brink of an orgasm. Jesus, she felt as if she were with two different men. One was her familiar best friend, while the other was a hot, dominant stranger who made her want to do all sorts of nasty, naughty things.

"We *are* going to have a honeymoon, Riley. Make no mistake about it. When we come back to this room, I'm going to lay you across that bed and come inside that sweet body of yours until we both pass out from exhaustion. Got it?" He punctuated his question with a hard, quick kiss that took her breath away.

When he stepped away, he'd turned back into her affable, easygoing friend once more. "Come on. Let's go find Trev."

CHAPTER THREE

R iley and Aaron took a quick cruise through the slot machines in the hotel, hoping they'd get lucky and run in to Trevor.

"You realize finding Trev in Vegas is going to be harder than finding an all-you-can-eat buffet for under twenty bucks," Riley grumbled.

"I know. Hey, there's the dealer from your blackjack table last night. Let's talk to him."

"I played blackjack?"

Aaron chuckled. "You were winning too."

"Oh yeah? Awesome."

They approached the dealer and Aaron noticed the man recognized Riley right away. "Welcome back, Riley. Did you come to try your luck again?"

Riley shook her head, undaunted that the man knew her name. Riley was infamous for making friends everywhere she went, but Aaron was going to have a serious talk with her about her partying habits of late.

Typically she knew how to have a good time and what her limits were. This weekend binge of hers drove home to him how depressed she must have been lately. She wasn't usually quite so reckless.

"No. Actually I'm looking for Trevor, the guy I was with yesterday."

"Ah, Bella's date," the dealer said.

She nodded. "Have you seen them lately?"

The man shook his head. "Not since last night. Your friend hit the jackpot on the Money Madness machine. After that, he and Bella took off."

"He hit the jackpot?" Riley asked.

"One hundred grand."

"Shut. Up. Trevor won a hundred thousand dollars? That lucky bastard." Riley shook her head in disbelief.

Aaron shrugged, unsurprised. Money always seemed to fall into Trev's lap. He'd matched four numbers in the lottery once, found five hundred dollars in a coffee can on the street, and inherited a few thousand from an uncle he didn't even know he had. Problem was, the money never stayed in Trev's pocket for long. "He does seem to be doing pretty well for himself in Vegas."

The dealer obviously agreed. "I'll say. Winning all that money *and* spending the evening with Bella." The man's look let them know exactly which part of Trev's good fortune he preferred.

Aaron chuckled as Riley rolled her eyes. "It's a big-tit epidemic," she muttered.

"Thanks for your help." Aaron led Riley back

toward the front desk of the hotel, where they introduced themselves and asked about the staff working the previous night's shift. The reservation clerk said the same crew would be working that night. Riley and Aaron decided if they still hadn't found Trev by then, they would come back to question them all later.

Aaron took her hand and led her away from the desk. "So it sounds like Trevor and Bella won a bunch of money and split."

"Knowing Trev, he decided this hotel was beneath him once he got a few bucks in his pocket."

"Probably," Aaron agreed. "Bella certainly looked like the type who wouldn't mind helping a fella blow all his hard-earned money."

"So the only words I heard in that comment were Bella, blow and hard," Riley joked.

"Touché."

Riley's cell phone went off, the sounds of *Brick House* surrounding them. He chuckled at her ring tone as she pulled the phone out of her purse and looked at the caller ID.

She sighed. "Shit."

"Who is it?"

"Tris." She continued to let the phone ring.

"Aren't you going to answer it?"

She shook her head. The phone stopped ringing and she began to count backward. "Five, four, three, two, one." As she hit one, the phone started ringing again. "Jeez, he's relentless."

"Give me the phone." Aaron snatched the cell out of her hands.

"Hey," she protested, but he was quicker. He clicked with one hand while fending her off with the other.

"Hello," he said.

"Aaron?"

"Yeah, it's me."

"I assume, since you're on Riley's phone, you found her." Tristan's voice betrayed his irritation toward his baby sister.

Aaron looked at Riley, who was glaring at him with her arms crossed against her chest. He let his gaze drift to her breasts, nicely accentuated by her pose. He wiggled his eyebrows.

"Pervert," she muttered, taking her arms down and turning her back on him.

"I found her," he said into the phone.

"When are you coming home?" Tris asked.

"We're going to hang out in Vegas for a few days."

Tris went quiet on the other end for a few moments. "There's a funny rumor flying around here today."

"It's true," Aaron said.

He could hear Tristan's sharp intake of breath. "You and Riley are *married?*"

"Yep. Soon as we track down Trevor, we're going to start our honeymoon."

Riley spun around at his words, fury evident on her face. *"What are you doing?"*

"Telling your family our good news." He knew his response would send her into orbit, but he refused to back down on this subject. If he gave Riley an inch she'd take a mile and he wasn't budging on their marriage. She was his wife and she was damn well going to stay his wife. It was time she accepted that.

"Listen, Tris. Do you mind letting everyone know? I'm sorry about springing it on you this way, but it was sort of a surprise to us too."

"Didn't expect you to go to such lengths when I asked you to take care of her." Aaron recalled Tris and Ewan pulling him aside after Teagan's wedding and asking him to keep an eye on her. He knew of all her siblings, Tris worried about Riley the most.

"Listen, we'll have a big party when we get back. Celebrate in style."

Tris laughed. "Sounds like a plan. Welcome to the family, bro, and, um…good luck. You'll need it."

Aaron smiled as he hung up the phone. He'd grown up with the Collins siblings and they'd never failed to make him feel like part of the family. Realizing he was suddenly an official member made him happier than he would have expected.

He looked at his new wife, shooting daggers at him, and realized Tris was right. He was going to need luck —lots of it. "You were right. Johanna's apparently been making a few calls home."

"And rather than deny it, you told Tris we were married. Knowing perfectly well that I don't want to *stay* married."

Aaron narrowed his eyes warningly. "What you want and what you need are two different things right now. It won't always be that way."

"When did you get so stubborn?"

He reached over and pulled her toward him, silently rejoicing when, rather than fight him, she moved into him, accepting his embrace and wrapping her arms around his waist. "When something is really important to me, I go after it. I don't think that makes me stubborn. Just determined."

She rested her cheek against his chest and tightened her hold. "You're going to be sorry about this one day. I'm not easy to live with."

He chuckled. "Riley, I've been a part of your life for over twenty years and I've never wanted to leave. I don't see that changing anytime in the near future."

She stepped back and looked at him. Her eyes seemed to study every feature on his face and he wondered what she was thinking. Then she rose up on her tiptoes, pulling his head down to hers.

"You're crazy," she whispered. For the first time since they'd woken up married, she initiated a kiss. He let her lead the way, her lips betraying the conflicting emotions inside her. At first her kiss was soft, tentative, but within moments it became hard, needy, rough. She nipped his lower lip with her teeth and a growl rumbled in his throat.

His cock had never been this hard for this long. He was beginning to fear for his health. Sustaining an erection for hours on end couldn't be a good thing. What did those warnings on the commercials for Viagra say? Four hours? No way would the doctors in the emergency room believe his was all natural.

Her tongue touched his and he realized if he didn't

break this off, he'd throw her down on the floor of the hotel lobby and give the gamblers a show.

"Riley." He grasped her wrists, pulling them away from his neck. "We have to stop, sweetheart. Too many more of those kisses and we'll both be arrested for indecent exposure."

She opened her eyes. "Just for kissing?"

"It's what your kisses make me want to do that could get us into trouble."

She gave him a sexy grin. "Oh yeah?"

"Yeah. I'm two minutes away from yanking those tight jeans of yours down and bending you over the check-in counter." Her eyes darkened, letting him know she wouldn't resist just such an occurrence, and he groaned. "Jesus."

"I'm starting to think Trev can go hang."

"Your headache?" he asked.

"Miraculously gone. The room's only three flights up."

He reached for her hand. Trevor was on his own.

"Excuse me," the registration clerk called out. They turned to see the man waving them over. "Did you say your name was Riley Collins?"

"Yes," Riley said.

"I completely forgot. You have a message. Perhaps it's from your friend."

"Hallelujah." She took the slip of paper from the man. "Do you know when this was left?"

"Some time last night. It was here this morning when I came into work," the clerk replied.

"What does it say?" Aaron asked.

"Says he doesn't need his return-flight ticket. Shit." Riley looked at his wrist. "Do you have a watch? What time is it?"

"A little after two."

"Damn. So much for the plane tickets. My flight left at one-thirty."

"You weren't flying home today regardless," Aaron said. "Honeymoon boom-boom, remember? What else did Trev say?"

Riley skimmed the note and cursed.

"He's not going back to Baltimore. Says he and Bella are going to get married."

"He's already married," Aaron said.

"Yeah, well, brainiac Trev has apparently forgotten that little fact."

"Johanna will flip out." Aaron glanced over his shoulder, afraid saying the woman's name would conjure her out of thin air. "I guess it's a good thing Trev decided to pull this shit out of town. There's no way Jo got any of her hunting rifles on the plane."

"Yeah, but it's Vegas. What do you think the chances are she could buy a gun…or ten?"

Aaron frowned. "I don't want to be the one to break this news to her. The woman is unstable on a good day. Pregnancy isn't going to help that. Besides, if she starts crying again—"

"Well, don't look at me. That crazy bitch already tried to take my head off today with a baseball bat."

"So the game plan stays the same. We find Trev."

Riley sighed. "I knew you were going to say that."

"She's having the man's baby. They deserve a chance to work out their differences, Riley."

"You know, this 'protect and defend' philosophy you live by really gives me a pain sometimes."

"You love me and you know it."

"I guess so, but this honeymoon totally sucks so far."

He laughed, pleased to see her beginning to soften toward the idea of their marriage. "I'll make it up to you. Promise."

"So, Mr. Responsible, where to now? Seems to me we've hit a wall."

"Not really." Aaron took the note from Riley's hand and pointed to the logo on the stationary.

"Sal's Sex Shop? You aren't planning to visit Sal, are you?"

"Worth checking it out and we can kill two birds with one stone," he said.

Her eyes narrowed suspiciously. "What's that supposed to mean?"

"You insulted my honeymoon."

"So?"

"So maybe a few fun wedding gifts will make you feel better about being married to me."

She gave him a naughty grin and he knew he was the luckiest man alive.

"Maybe they will," she said.

THE SEX SHOP was within walking distance of the hotel. As they stood outside, Riley studied the small storefront with disdain. All the windows were covered with black paper and a cheap, blue neon light displayed the store's name.

"Classy joint," she mumbled.

Aaron opened the door and they stepped into the dimly lit shop. There was only one other customer in the place and Aaron decided the store was similar to every sex shop he'd ever been in. As a police officer, it wasn't unusual for him to have to check out complaints about indecent exposure and the like at places just like this back home. "He doesn't look like a Sal to me." He pointed to the pimply faced young guy sitting behind the counter.

"Yep, it's a safe bet he's earning minimum wage, not top billing."

Aaron nodded as the clerk flipped the page of his magazine. "Well, there are still perks to the job. He can look at all the nudie magazines he wants for free."

"Some perk," Riley said distractedly. He followed her as she walked down an aisle, looking at all the sex toys. He loved how she could step into any situation or place and never have trouble fitting in. Most women he knew would never dream of stepping into a store like this, but Riley didn't even blink twice as she picked up the largest dildo he'd ever seen and waved it at him.

"What woman could possibly think this would be fun?"

He shrugged, picking up a neon green dildo. "Prob-ably the same woman who would want to play with a green cock. You think it's some sort of environmental statement? Go green?"

"Hey." She took the dildo from him. "That's kind of cool. Wonder if it glows in the dark."

He chuckled. "Move along, Mrs. Young. Your dildo days are done. I've got your cock right here." He grasped her hand and let her feel his re-emerging erection.

She snorted but left her hand on him. "Glow in the dark is pretty hard to compete with. You think you're up for it?"

Her comment certainly moved him further into the *up* position and she giggled as his cock thickened in her palm. "Guess that answers that." She patted him lightly before walking away.

He closed his eyes and prayed he'd be able to follow. She was killing him.

"Vibrators could be fun," she announced.

He nodded and took two painful steps toward her. She was bent over looking at the rabbit varieties, her ass taunting him. Coming to a sex shop when he was this horny was dumber than going to the grocery store hungry.

He bypassed her vibrators, his interest lying else-where. "This one," he said, picking up a slim vibrator and handing it to her. "We're getting this one."

"Why?" She looked at his selection.

"Remote control."

She laughed. "The ultimate guy accessory. Okay. Looks like fun."

She continued walking and he noticed she'd picked

up her pace. Glancing at the nearest shelves, he understood—and realized with glee he'd found a chink in his girl's armor.

"Hey." He grasped her hand and dragged her back to the shelves she'd just sped by. "You're missing the best stuff."

She raised a haughty eyebrow at him when she saw where his gaze had landed. "No. Way." She enunciated both words clearly.

"Hell. Yes." He mimicked her tone, grinning when she flushed. "Are you telling me, Riley Collins, that I've actually found something you've never done?"

"I'm not talking to you about this. It's personal."

Aaron laughed. "We're married. Nothing's personal anymore. You mean to tell me you aren't a little bit curious?"

"That particular place is an exit, not an entrance. I plan for it to stay that way."

He reached over to pick up a small butt plug. "We'll work up to it." He grabbed a tube of lubrication as well.

"Oh no, we won't."

He nodded, placing his hand on her back and directing her around the corner to the next aisle.

"You're wasting your money on those things." She pointed to the plug and lube.

He didn't bother responding.

"You're being stubborn again," she added.

"Determined," he replied.

"Annoying."

"Is this some sort of name game?" he joked.

She glanced at the shelf behind him and an evil look crossed her face. He braced himself. Riley may get knocked down, but she never got knocked out. "Okay, if you're buying those, I want *these*." She picked up handcuffs.

"Sweetheart, I'm a cop. I've got at least a half-dozen pairs of those at home. And believe me, I'm more than willing to use all of them on you."

"Oh, they're not for me. They're for you."

He narrowed his eyes. Riley may know him as an easygoing friend, content to follow in her wake, but in the bedroom he liked to direct. She'd reacted to and assimilated that fact all morning. She liked it when he took charge. He could see it.

He tried to figure out the best way to proceed. He could see the blade of the guillotine poised over his head and his answer now could signal reprieve or death.

"You want to tie me up?"

She nodded.

Aaron leaned closer as he whispered his next question. "And what would you do with me once you had me at your mercy?"

"I have this fantasy," she began with a smile and he wondered what he'd set himself up for.

"I'm in this empty room and there's a gorgeous, naked guy standing in the middle of it with his arms chained above his head. Usually the guy is Ryan Reynolds, but I guess you'll do."

"Very funny." He pictured himself bare-assed and bound in her room.

"Anyway, you're completely helpless. I can do anything I want to you."

He swallowed heavily and watched the guy in the next aisle take a couple steps closer to them. Great, she was attracting an audience in a sex shop. Typical Riley.

"I walk around you a few times, just touching you here and there." She imitated her words with glancing brushes on his arm, his shoulder, the top of his thigh. "You're rock-hard and aching for me, but I've warned you not to speak. If you talk—even to beg—I'll leave."

He knew it was just a fantasy, but for some reason he felt as if she'd just forbidden him to speak. The clerk behind the counter put his magazine down and looked up.

"I know you want me to touch your cock. I can see you pleading with your eyes, but you're my toy and I'm not about to let the game end too soon. I move to stand behind you. You start to turn your head but I say no. You have to look forward."

She moved into the position as she spoke and he only just stopped turning his head to look at her. The man in the next aisle had stopped pretending to shop and was now watching Riley, hanging on her every word. Fuck, so was Aaron for that matter.

"I run my hands along your back. I love your back, you know. So muscular and sexy. I love to watch you mow grass in the summer. Love to see you with your shirt off and sweat running down your tanned skin. So hot."

Her fingers traced lines on the back of his shirt and he imagined she was touching the slick moisture. "I can sense how badly you want me, so I decide to offer you a small reward for your good behavior. I reach down and cup your ass, squeezing hard." Her hand drifted down to touch his ass and he wished she would grab it like she'd described.

"I run my finger along the crevice there and tell you to spread your legs."

He swallowed heavily. She moved forward to whisper her next words and out of the corner of his eye, he saw the customer and the clerk both lean closer to hear. "You obey because you're such a *good* boy." Her breath tickled and her words rankled a bit. She'd always given him hell for being too good, too perfect. The fact she thought he'd toe her line in the bedroom irritated him.

It was also a challenge. She was testing him. He grinned.

"I touch your ass, grip your balls from behind. You moan a little but I don't punish you for it." Her hand hovered on his denim-clad ass. He remained quiet. Biding his time.

"When I decide I can't wait any longer, I move around to face you." She walked to stand in front of him and ran her hand down his chest. Her eyes sparkled with mischief and she spoke louder. Oh yeah, she knew they had an audience. "You want to beg me, but you won't."

"You're right," he said. "I won't beg." He could see he'd surprised her by speaking. She narrowed her eyes. "I look right at you and tell you you've had your fun. I tell you it's my turn and I command you to get on your knees."

"Command?" He could tell she wanted to be offended, but her nipples had hardened beneath her T-shirt and he could hear her breathing accelerate.

"You obey," he said, "because you've always been a very *naughty* girl."

She grinned. "So I have."

"Should I tell you how the fantasy ends?" he asked.

She looked around and acknowledged their audience. "Sorry guys," she announced. "I think my husband and I are going to have to wrap this one up alone."

Aaron tried to ignore the pleasure he felt at hearing her call him *husband*.

"Damn. Fucking hot fantasy. Lucky son of a bitch," the customer said, looking at Aaron.

Riley smiled appreciatively at the man's compliment and grabbed a pair of handcuffs, daring Aaron to say something as she headed for the register. He dropped his purchases next to hers and struggled not to gloat. She was oozing arousal from every pore and suffering for it. Good. Woman had kept him in a state of constant horniness for hours. Payback was a bitch.

"Hey," he said to the clerk as he rang up the items. "Were you working here last night too?"

The clerk nodded. "Yeah, today was supposed to be my day off, but the stupid bitch who works the day shift called in sick…again. Third time this month."

"You didn't happen to see a burly-looking guy and

a blonde woman in a sequin dress, did you?" Aaron figured it was a long shot, but he was out of ideas.

"You mean Bella?" the clerk asked.

Riley perked up. "Yeah. She was out with a friend of ours and we're trying to track them down."

"Tourist? Camouflage jacket? Receding hairline?" The clerk bagged their purchases as he spoke.

"That's our friend." Aaron handed over his credit card.

"They were in here looking at the pony girl stuff, but they didn't buy anything."

"Pony girl?" Riley asked.

"Yeah, it's when the girl sticks a tail up her—"

"I know what it is," Riley interrupted. "Just didn't realize Trev was into that kind of thing." She turned to Aaron. "I'm starting to think Jo might be better off if we don't find him."

"Oh, I don't think he was all that interested," the clerk replied. "That pony girl game is Bella's thing. She's bought stuff in here before. Your friend actually looked a little scared when she talked about it. Kinda funny."

Aaron chuckled. Trev was getting a hell of an education with the hooker. "Why didn't they buy anything?"

"Bubbles showed up."

"Bubbles?" Riley and Aaron asked in unison.

"She's a ho, works the street. She and Bella are kinda arch enemies. You know, like Superman and Lex Luthor."

Aaron glanced down. The guy was reading a

comic. So much for taking advantage of the perks of working in a sex shop.

"So what happened?" Riley asked.

"Nothing. I nipped it. Told 'em to take it outside. Those two are always fighting. It's sort of a regular event around here, so most us know to move them out of the store pretty damn quick whenever they end up in the same place at the same time. Otherwise, shit gets broken and I can tell you right now, it ain't coming outta *my* paycheck."

"You don't happen to know where they went when they left, do you?" he asked.

"Nah. They left and nothing got busted up. That's all I cared about. I know Bubbles was pissed as shit at Bella for something. She was cussing a blue streak, following them down the street."

"Do you know where we can find Bubbles?" Aaron asked.

"You're going to look for Bubbles? Jesus H. Christ." Riley closed her eyes and he suspected she was praying for patience. Clearly her prayers had not been answered.

"She was the last one to see Trev. We're following a trail, Riley. This is standard police work. Welcome to my world."

"You a cop?" the clerk asked.

"Not at the moment," he answered quickly. "I'm on my honeymoon."

"That's cool." The young guy grinned and pointed out the door. "Bubbles will be on that corner over there in about an hour. She's partial to animal-print tops, but they ain't partial to her. Oh, and she's got pink hair this week."

Aaron picked up their bag of goodies and led Riley back out onto the street. "Sounds like we've got a little bit of time to kill. Sweaty sex or late lunch?"

She looked at him for a few moments, appearing so torn he had to stifle his laughter. "If we have sex, it's like I'm admitting we're married."

"We *are* married, Riley. You just called me your husband in there."

"Yeah well, I'm not totally ready to declare defeat yet."

He put his arm around her shoulder and kissed the top of her head. "Late lunch it is then."

CHAPTER FOUR

After a very late lunch, Riley and Aaron headed back to the spot where the clerk at Sal's said they would find Bubbles. They'd nearly reached the corner when Riley stopped mid-stride.

"Holy shit," she muttered, her gaze falling on Bubbles.

Aaron had gone two steps farther when he spotted the woman as well and halted.

"Jesus," he said.

Riley stood rooted to the spot, blinking several times. The clerk hadn't been lying about Bubbles' love of animal prints, but she hadn't really fully appreciated his joke about them not loving her until this moment.

Aaron walked back toward her. "Wow." His grin proved he was enjoying Riley's reaction.

Riley looked at him and shook her head in disbelief. "Tit Mecca."

"Oh yeah," he agreed. "Not sure I've ever seen…"

His words faded away unfinished as he turned to look at the hooker again.

"That woman has managed to squeeze her 34DDD boobs into an extra-small shirt. It's like…"

"Like she's defying gravity," Aaron finished for her. "The animal print certainly accentuates her…"

"Her everything."

Riley studied Bubbles, prying her eyes away from the woman's chest to take in the rest of her. She was tall, close to six feet—not including her hair, which added at least another three or four inches to her towering frame. Her hair was long, teased to within an inch of its life and—as they'd been warned—pink. Hot pink. Her dark skin and eyes betrayed her Hispanic heritage and she was wearing a wildly patterned spandex shirt that barely contained her girls.

Riley could now understand the woman's nick-name. Her "bubbles" were very impressive, given the fact the woman possessed such a lanky frame. She wasn't sure how Bubbles was remaining upright with all that weight in front. She had on super-tight pants that outlined her shapely ass and legs, and strangely, despite her crazy outfit and hair, Riley considered Bubbles one of the most beautiful women she'd ever seen.

Aaron turned to face her again and from the corner of her eye, she saw his smile grow.

"You doing okay, Riley?"

She narrowed her eyes. "Think I just got my first serious girl crush."

He laughed. "On Bubbles? Jesus, I'm gonna have to

get you out of Vegas soon. You're starting to fit in here."

"Didn't know this place was Titty City. Don't you think she looks sort of hot?"

"I'm trying to look at her face, Riley, I swear to God. It's just—those boobs. It's like a train wreck. I can't make myself look away."

She laughed. "Men. So typical. Come on. Let's see if she knows where Bella is."

They approached the woman as she appeared to be offering her services to a tiny bald man who was sweating profusely.

"Excuse me," Riley said. Bubbles turned. The hooker's gaze landed on Riley for a split second before it flew to Aaron.

"Well, now. Hello there," Bubbles purred at Aaron. Riley grinned as her new husband blushed under the hooker's intense scrutiny. Bubbles looked back at the bald man, dismissing him. "Sorry honey. Just got a better offer. Adios."

As she spoke, she wiggled her fingers in a short wave. The bald man sighed heavily before walking away. Riley felt sorry for the poor man who looked as if his beloved puppy had just been run over by a truck.

"I think you may have misunderstood," Aaron said, trying to warn Bubbles she was sending away her paycheck. "We're not here to, um..." He looked at Riley for help and she laughed at the utter panic on his face.

"My friend isn't propositioning you for sex," Riley explained.

Bubbles grinned and Riley sucked in a breath. The woman had perfect white teeth, and again she was struck by her beauty.

Shit. She *was* going loopy in this freaking city.

"Maybe he'd like a sample before he throws away what I'm offering." Bubbles took a step closer—all that was required to leave her chest a hairsbreadth away from Aaron.

"Miss, um—" Aaron started.

"Bubbles, *bebé*. Everybody calls me Bubbles." As she spoke, she thrust her bubbles closer, her erect nipples brushing against Aaron's T-shirt. He took a giant step back but Bubbles was undaunted, following him. Riley fought back the laughter Aaron's terrified face stirred in her.

"Bubbles." Riley tried to draw the woman's attention toward her in an attempt to save Aaron. "Hello, over here," she said, waving her hands.

Bubbles turned and Riley sensed it was the first time the woman really saw her. "You can play too, *chica*. There's plenty of Bubbles to go around."

"I can see that," Riley said, "but we're really not interested in sex."

The hooker narrowed her eyes in disbelief. "Oh, you can't lie to Bubbles, *chica*. You expect me to believe you're walking around with this sexy number and you're *not* thinking about gettin' in that big boy's pants? Sell that shit to somebody else."

Riley glanced at Aaron and had to admit the woman had a point. She was so hot for him, she felt as if she could spontaneously combust on the spot.

Jesus, when did life become so complicated? She'd spent twenty years with Aaron and never felt a ripple of desire. Now it was as if every wasted second of the past two decades was crashing in on her at once and she needed to fuck him or die in the attempt.

She tore her attention away from Aaron, who was now grinning delightedly since Bubbles' attention had turned toward her.

Revenge was such a sweet thing.

"Oh Bubbles, the dirty, nasty things I want to do with Aaron and *to* Aaron would make *you* blush. I just think it's more correct to say we're not interested in a threesome."

Aaron groaned at her words and Riley laughed when he adjusted his jeans. "Dammit, Riley," he muttered.

Bubbles' eyebrows rose and Riley suspected she'd earned the woman's respect. "Don't knock it 'til you've tried it, sweetheart."

Riley considered her comment for a moment and then glanced at Aaron. A threesome might be fun.

"No," he said quickly, obviously seeing where Riley's thoughts had wandered.

Bubbles turned her attention back to him, but before she could speak, Aaron cut her off. "My wife and I are here on our honeymoon," he told her. "Hell, I haven't even had a chance to have sex with *her* yet, so you can both forget the threesome thing."

The hooker turned to her. "You married this guy and you haven't even had sex with each other yet? Risky."

Riley had to agree. She hadn't considered it until this moment. What if the sex sucked? "She's got a point."

He shook his head. "We'll set the sheets on fire, Riley, and you know it. Could we try to keep the conversation on track? Trev," he reminded her.

"We're looking for a friend of ours," she said to Bubbles. "The clerk at Sal's said he saw you talking to him and his date last night."

"I don't know anybody named Trev," Bubbles replied.

"Yeah, but I think you know his date. Her name is Bella."

Bubbles went off like a bottle rocket. "That cunt! That whore! How dare you say that bitch's name to me!"

Riley threw her hands up in surrender when Bubbles took a menacing step toward her. "Hey, I'm just looking for Trev. I've never even met this Bella bimbo."

"That's not completely true," Aaron muttered and Riley shot him a dirty look.

"In case you've forgotten, I was drunk last night. I don't remember *anything*." She stressed *anything* and a scowl crossed his face.

"Remember or not, the things that happened last night *still* happened and trying to avoid the truth—"

"Um, hello," Bubbles interjected, "but I don't know what the fuck you two are talking about."

"Sorry." Riley threw a nasty glance in Aaron's direction. "Our friend Trev hooked up with—"

"The cunt." Bubbles interrupted her with the nasty nickname and Riley grinned at the sound of it. She'd never used the word as a curse before, but she had to admit it had a certain ring to it.

"Forget it," Aaron said, stepping up behind Riley.

"What?"

"Forget you ever heard that word. I know you. You'll start flinging it around as easily as you do the food at the pub. Your pop hears that and he'll wash your mouth out with soap and then blame me for letting you use it."

"You have to admit it has a certain pizzazz."

"It's vulgar and crude and you're an aunt. Erase it from your mind right now."

"Spoilsport," Riley muttered.

"Are you two on fucking drugs or something? What the fuck is wrong with you?" Bubbles asked.

Aaron stepped forward. "Trev ran off last night with—"

Bubbles started to interject her nasty nickname for Bella, but Aaron cut her off.

"With Bella," he said loudly. "Trev's wife has shown up in Vegas now and she'd like her husband back. We told her we'd track him down for her."

Bubbles' head swayed sideways and Riley fought not to laugh at the woman's haughty expression. "Hmpf. You might wanna tell that wife her two-timing husband has dipped his stick in a well of STD-infested poison. I wouldn't take a man back who'd fucked Bella even if he'd been dunked in a vat of bleach and scrubbed off with twenty-two cases of Purell."

"Lovely imagery," Riley muttered.

"We'll pass your advice along to Trev's wife, but for now, we really just need to find him," Aaron said.

Riley was impressed with his calm, matter-of-fact manner. In the meantime, she was hungover, horny and torn between laughing her ass off or curling into a fetal position and crying her eyes out. She was going to knock every tooth Trev had left down his throat when she found him. Nobody was worth this much hassle.

"I don't have any clue where the cunt is and I don't really care to know."

"Fine," Aaron said. "Thank you for your time."

He took Riley's hand and turned to leave, but Bubbles stopped him. "You could always ask Johnny."

"Johnny?" Riley asked.

"Johnny Sparks, Bella's old man. If she's run off with this friend of yours, you can be damn sure Johnny's looking for them too. You better hope you find them first or there won't be too many parts of your friend left *to* find."

"Any idea where we could find this Johnny guy?" The question seemed to be pulled from Aaron's gut and Riley could appreciate the sentiment. The idea of tracking down Bella's pimp, especially if he was dangerous, didn't seem like such a good idea.

"He hangs out at Jacko's—closes it down every night, the drunk asshole. It's a bar on the edge of town. Kind of a rough place." Bubbles looked at Riley as she spoke and Riley appreciated the woman's warning.

"What does he look like?" Aaron asked. "Might help us find him if we have a description."

Bubbles laughed. "Oh, *bebé*. You don't gotta worry 'bout that. You can't miss Johnny Sparks. He thinks he's fucking Wayne Newton. Dresses like him, looks like him, acts like him. Shame he can't sing like him. Maybe he wouldn't be such a loser then. Stuck with cunts like Bella."

"Thanks for the help, Bubbles. Listen…" Riley pulled a tattered receipt and pen from her purse. "Here's my cell number. If you see Bella again, do you mind giving me a call?"

Bubbles took the number and nodded. "I'll call you right after I beat her silicone-infested jugs into the ground."

"Why do you hate Bella so much?" Riley asked, curiosity getting the better of her.

"Cunt knows this block is my territory. She went into that casino and picked up your friend knowing he shoulda been my john. Then he wins that jackpot and she's flitting all over town acting like a big shot. He was my Richard Gere."

Riley was confused. "Richard Gere."

"Didn't you ever see the movie *Pretty Woman*? Rich guy falls for the hooker. Saves her from a life on the streets by proposing."

"Trev isn't rich," Riley explained. "And he's already married. I'm pretty sure he doesn't qualify for the Richard Gere role."

Bubbles shrugged and then laughed. "Then maybe I'll let Bella live, just so I can laugh at her sorry ass when she realizes her Prince Charming is a frog."

Riley nodded.

"I'll tell you this," Bubbles said. "Last time Bella ran off with a guy, Johnny put a hit on him. You find your friend, you'd be smart to get him and his wife outta Vegas."

"That's the plan," Riley agreed. "Thanks again, Bubbles."

"Sure thing, *chica*. You ever convince your man to play at the threesome, you come find me. I'll give you two the full-service deal for free."

Riley glanced at Aaron, who was shaking his head.

"Free," she said with a laugh as he wrapped his arm across her shoulders and led her back to the hotel.

"Dammit, Riley. Can I get into *your* pants first before we start exploring ways to jazz up our nonexistent sex life?"

She shrugged, not ready to let go of the joke. "I guess so. Just seems to me you don't get an offer like that every day, sugar."

"I'm not worried," he assured her. "I've known you forever and believe me, those sex offers come your way all the time."

She laughed. "Like when?"

"Like when Bobby Arthur offered you twelve dollars to touch your boobs in middle school."

"Twelve bucks was a lot of money in middle school."

"Like when Jules Rodgers came out of the closet our junior year and announced to everyone she was in love with you," he added.

"Well, now I'll admit that was awkward. But we're fine now. She's still a really good friend."

Aaron rolled his eyes. "All I'm saying is it's not that unusual for people to offer you sex in whatever variety or form."

"Everyone except you."

He frowned. "What's that mean?"

"It means that until this morning, you've never even hinted at being interested in me sexually. Don't you find that odd?"

He shook his head. "Not really. I knew it was all or nothing with you. I've always known that."

"All or nothing?"

"I would never have been able to have sex with you, Riley, without wanting a committed relationship, without wanting marriage as the end result. Until last night, that never seemed like a possibility."

"What happened last night?"

He grinned. "You let the mask slip."

She paused to consider his comment. Had she revealed the reason she'd been so depressed lately? Had she confessed her secret desire to get married? Obviously she had, hence her current dilemma. "I'm never drinking again."

"You always say that. This too shall pass."

As they approached their hotel, they paused outside. It was early evening and Riley's energy level was nearly depleted. It had been a long day. Hell, it had been a long weekend and it was showing no signs of slowing up. "What now?"

"Let's cruise through the casino again. It's probably too early for Johnny to be at the bar. I figure we have a fifty-fifty chance he's a mean drunk."

"You want to wait until he's drunk *and* mean?"

"No," Aaron said. "I want the other fifty percent. Drunk enough to be helpful and harmless."

"You do realize our luck in this godforsaken city hasn't been all that great so far."

Aaron smiled. "Are you kidding? I'm having the luckiest weekend of my life and I'm about to hit the jackpot."

She narrowed her eyes suspiciously. "How so?"

"After we determine Trev isn't hanging out by the slot machines, I'm taking you up to the room and making you my wife. Once and for all."

RILEY PULLED her sweater over her head as they entered the hotel room. Aaron had pushed buttons in her she didn't know she had.

Fuck it.

She was having sex with him and to hell with the consequences. The sound of leather swishing against denim proved Aaron was in a hurry too as his belt hit the floor. He kicked the door shut with his foot as he reached out for her, turning and pushing her against it.

"Haven't I seen you here before?" She recalled they'd been in the exact same position this morning.

Aaron grinned. "Same place, different ending. Take off your clothes."

"I'd rather take yours off." She reached for his T-shirt, pulling it over his head, her heart racing at the sight of his bare chest. She'd seen the man shirtless a thousand times in the past, but for some inexplicable reason, she felt as if she was seeing it clearly for the first time and a strange sense of possessiveness gripped her.

He was hers.

She leaned forward to kiss him, her lips grazing his pecs before cruising over to visit his nipple. She ran her tongue around the tiny bud as Aaron's hands gripped her waist. She could sense his growing need. Hell, she shared it. She wasn't an innocent, not even close. But for some reason, this time with Aaron felt as if she would be losing her virginity all over again. She pulled away from his chest to look at him, her breathing ragged.

She was inundated by so many emotions, she was finding it hard to know what to do next. She wanted him. There was no question of that, but while her body was urging her to claim and conquer, her head was warning her to proceed with caution. Overpowering all of that was her heart, screaming at her not to fuck this up. Proclaiming loud and clear she'd finally gotten something right.

Aaron offered her a crooked grin and kissed her forehead. "Never pegged you as a thinker, Riley. Always saw you as more of a doer." His taunt hit the nail square on the head, just as he'd known it would, and she narrowed her eyes before unhooking her bra and sliding it off.

"I thought I'd better take it slow for you, sugar. Don't wanna overwhelm you." She cupped her breasts, toying with the tight nipples with her own fingers. "Think you can keep up?"

He growled. *Jesus, a growl?* She didn't have more than a second to process that thought before his lips descended on her breasts. He brushed her hands aside, grasping her breasts, holding them still for his assault. There was no part of her chest left untouched as he licked around her areolas, lightly bit her nipples, kissed the sensitive skin and massaged the plump flesh.

"God." She wondered where the hell Aaron had learned to play like this. She'd always imagined sex with him would be staid, gentle…boring. Where had this tit connoisseur come from?

She shook the thought from her head. This was going too fast, getting too serious. She felt completely off balance and grasped the only thing she could still call on to work in her defense. "Hope you aren't disappointed," she joked. "I'm no Bubbles."

He sucked her taut nipple into his mouth…hard, the suction producing a pleasurable pain she'd never experienced. Her head fell back against the door, thudding loudly against the wood.

He moved upward from her breasts, planting hot, wet kisses along her neck. "It won't work," he whispered into her ear.

"What won't work?"

"The jokes. I'm not stopping and neither are you."

"Who's asking you to stop?" She gripped his hair with her fingers, holding his mouth to her neck. She loved having her neck kissed. He moved, taking her earlobe between his teeth, biting it lightly while his fingers pinched her nipples and she trembled under his forceful, sexy-as-shit attack.

"Still with me, Riley? Didn't leave you in the dust, did I?"

She grinned. *Smart-ass.* Jesus, she was going to make him pay for that.

She unbuttoned his jeans, taunting him with her eyes as she slid the zipper down. "You might want to pay attention." She knelt as she gripped the waistband of his jeans and boxers, pulling them down his thighs. "Maybe take some notes," she added as she dragged her tongue along his cock in one long lick. She looked up in time to see Aaron's palms land on the door, no doubt to hold himself up as she took the head of his cock into her mouth. Her gaze never left his as she sucked his hard flesh into her mouth.

"So fucking hot." He moved one hand to her head, tangling his fingers in her curls as he continued to praise her. "You're so goddamn gorgeous, Riley."

She smiled around his cock and he groaned when she took him deeper. Reaching down, she fondled his balls for a moment before exploring further, touching the tip of her index finger to his anus. He jerked and she almost lost her grip on his cock.

He took her head in his hands and pulled her away. "Bad girl." The heated look in his eyes contradicted his words.

"You started it," she said, alluding to his sex-store purchase.

He grinned. "And I'll finish it. Later." He reached down to help her up. "Take off your pants."

She quickly shed her jeans as Aaron kicked off his shoes and finished removing his pants. She started to walk toward the bed, but he surprised her by picking her up and carrying her.

"What are you doing?"

"I thought you might not remember me carrying you over the threshold last night. Thought I'd reenact it for you."

"You carried me over the threshold?"

"Of course I did, Mrs. Young."

She felt a lump form in her throat at his romantic gesture. She'd never thought herself susceptible to such mushy-gushy nonsense. She'd always been too practical, too cynical, but every word he said, every move he made cut straight to the heart of her and she found herself melting like a teenage girl with her first crush.

He placed her on the bed like she was made of glass and she fought to regain her composure. She'd spent the entire day fighting to return to common ground, struggling for some sense of normality only to have him rewrite the rules of their relationship time and time again. He lowered himself over her, their bare bodies touching from chest to feet. She could sense his strength—and his desire—and it lit her body on fire. She ran her hands along his back, savoring the deep kiss he offered.

When they broke apart for much-needed air, she realized resistance was futile. "Fuck me, Aaron."

He shook his head. "No. Our fucking days are over, Riley. I'm making love to you."

She wanted to roll her eyes, wanted to snort or do something completely like herself, but all she could do was nod and pray to keep the tears she felt clogging her throat from reaching her eyes. He reached to retrieve his pants but she halted him.

"No condom. I'm on birth control. Just us. Nothing in the way."

He considered her words for a moment and then grinned. "Just us. From now on." He leaned down to kiss her as she wrapped her legs around his waist. He nudged his cock against her pussy and she reached down to guide him home. He entered so slowly she wanted to protest, but his lips devoured any words she might have spoken. He wasn't lying about the making-love comment. Riley had never felt more cherished, more protected…more horny.

She pulled her lips away from his when he retreated just as slowly.

She started to complain, to demand he move, when she caught his mischievous gaze. He was teasing her.

Her honeymoon. Their first time together and he was making a damn joke.

She laughed. God, she loved him. "Had your fun?"

He shrugged. "Isn't this how you imagined sex with me would be?"

She frowned. "How the hell did you know that?"

"You told me so the night of Teagan's wedding. You'd had too much champagne and I foolishly mentioned that we'd never kissed."

She nodded, recalling her heartless reply. "You wanted to kiss me that night."

"It was midnight. New Year's. Besides, I've always wanted to kiss you. Always known—"

"That we were perfect for each other," she finished.

He grinned. "Yep."

"But that night, I said you and I could never be together romantically because we were too different."

"Because I was too boring and you were too wild." He repeated her reasoning.

"You aren't boring, Aaron. You've never been boring. I don't know why—"

"You were having a bad night, Riley. I understood."

She leaned up to kiss him. She'd been a bitch to him far too often in the past and he'd never left her side, never failed to support her. "I'm so sorry."

"You have nothing to be sorry about." His smile was easy, genuine. "I got my way in the end."

She laughed. "Because you're stubborn."

"Determined."

"Shut up and kiss me, sugar."

He bent down, his lips hard and possessive. His hips began to thrust and she marveled over the fact he'd been inside her the entire time they'd talked. It felt so natural. He began to move faster and she had to push away from his lips, gasp for air as he took complete ownership of her body. She tightened her legs around his waist, moaning when he reached down with one hand to touch her clit.

"Oh my God," she cried as he rubbed the sensitive, throbbing flesh. "So good."

He continued to pound inside her pussy, caressing her clit until she exploded in orgasm. She screamed at the incredible sensations pummeling her body but Aaron never wavered, dragging out the climax until she feared she'd pass out. As the feeling began to wane, she felt him pull out of her body.

"Roll over." His voice was deep, commanding, and she responded to it in an instant. "Hands and knees. I'm not finished with you."

She shivered at his hot words, surrendering control into his very capable hands. The moment she got into position, he was back inside her, his cock thrusting so deeply, she couldn't hold back her cries of delight. Within moments, she felt another climax building. Christ, he was going to kill her with all this pleasure. He reached around to grip her breasts, halting their movement as they swung under his forceful motions. He pinched her nipples while telling her all the dirty, lovely things he wanted to do to her.

His words—as much as his powerful fucking—pushed her over the edge again. Her body shuddered as it came down from the most intense orgasm of the century. She collapsed on her stomach, struggling to catch her breath.

"Not finished yet," Aaron whispered, kissing the nape of her neck.

"You're going to have to go on without me." Her words were muffled by the pillow. "Think I died halfway through that last orgasm."

He chuckled but remained undaunted. He rolled her onto her back. "One more, Riley," he insisted. "One more time, together."

He came over her once more, nudging her legs apart. This time he took her the way he'd promised at the beginning. His motions were slow, steady and loving, and her body embraced them. Every pulse of his cock teased her sensitive flesh, driving her to the peak. She'd never come this easily, this quickly.

Aaron thrust deeply one last time and she gave herself up to the feeling and to him. He cried out above her, his climax driving hers even higher.

"Love you," he said as his cock erupted inside her, filling her with his come. "God, I love you, Riley."

He lowered himself, pulling her toward his chest and enveloping her in his comforting embrace.

She didn't give him the words back. She couldn't. Her heart was too full of the emotion and it was spilling out everywhere. She wrapped her arm around his waist and fought back tears. She didn't cry. She never cried, but with his words and actions, he had claimed her heart, her soul, and she knew beyond a shadow of a doubt she would love him until the day she died. But she'd have to tell him tomorrow. Tonight, the sentiment was too strong.

Too potent.

Too new.

CHAPTER FIVE

Aaron jerked awake. Neon lights from the street below streamed through the sheer curtains, casting the room in an eerie pink haze. It took him several moments to remember where he was—Vegas—and what exactly had woken him up, and then he grinned.

"Trouble sleeping?" He was able to make out the top of Riley's head as it lowered toward his cock.

"You didn't let me finish earlier." She surrounded his engorged flesh with her mouth. Damn, the woman gave great head. He closed his eyes, struggling to keep from coming too soon. If this was any indication of how she intended to wake him up in the future, he was going to die a very happy man. He fought back a chuckle at the image of an elderly Riley going down on him when they were old and gray.

Her teeth grazed the sensitive spot beneath the head of his cock and he groaned. Her hand gripped the base of his dick tightly, moving in time with her mouth. Oh yeah, this wasn't going to take long. He'd spent too much of the day in a constant state of arousal to try to hold off the impending climax for too long.

Riley released his cock with a pop, looking up at him. "I'll let you choose," she said when he started to protest her abrupt end.

"Choose?"

"I can finish this blowjob until you come in my mouth or I can crawl on top of you and give you the ride of a lifetime." He stared at her for several moments until she giggled. "Trouble deciding?"

"I want both."

"Greedy bastard," she teased.

"Climb on, Riley. We'll see who enjoys the ride more."

"What about the blowjob?"

"Oh, I'll get that. Later. Don't worry. I'll let you know when."

She shook her head and he watched her grin grow as she straddled his hips. "Giddy up," she said with a laugh.

She slowly sank down on his cock and he fought the wave of lightheadedness that accompanied her movement. He gripped her hips and attempted to direct her motion, but he should have realized such an effort would be wasted. She paused, leaving him seated to the hilt, the heat of her pussy almost scalding.

"If you want me to continue, sugar, you have to follow my lead," she said. "Why don't we put those hands of yours to better use?" She grasped his hands, dragging them up to her breasts. "I know how much you like boobs."

He pinched her nipples in response, pleased by the sound of her sharp inhalation. "Don't get used to the driver's seat, Riley."

"Aaron—" she started, but he cut her off.

"I'm not a passive lover. We'll play this your way for now, but I don't make any promises that it will end with you in charge."

The muscles of her pussy fluttered against him. His comment seemed to knock her off balance for only a moment and then—as always—his girl recovered her equilibrium. He squeezed the globes of her breasts and she grinned, resuming her ride.

She took his cock inside her body like she lived her life—fast, hard, wild. It took all the strength he possessed not to come too soon. She knew exactly how to time the strokes, where to touch him to drive him mad, what to say to push him to the brink. Jesus, she was magnificent.

He moved his hands away from her breasts, savoring the smooth, soft texture of her skin. He skimmed his fingers along her waist to her hips before turning inward, toward her pussy. He delved between her legs, lightly caressing her clit with one finger before burrowing deeper. He rimmed the opening of her pussy, enjoying the feeling of her body taking his cock inside her. She gasped when he gathered some of the moisture created by their bodies and used it to rub her clit more deeply.

"God, I love that." She trembled as she spoke. He'd

learned earlier that she responded strongly when he stimulated her clit. Her pace increased as he pushed more firmly. She mimicked his motions as her arousal grew and took over. Her eyes were closed and he loved the complete rapture that covered her face a second before her orgasm claimed her. She was a vocal lover, her cries loud and lovely. As the climax reached its crescendo, she fell forward.

Wrapping his arms around her, he twisted them on the bed until she was beneath him, his cock still buried inside her. "Ready to hand me the reins?"

Her eyes opened at his request. "What did you have in mind?"

"I thought I'd surprise you."

She smiled. "I like surprises."

"I know." He reached for her legs, hooking his elbows in the crooks of her knees. "Feeling flexible?"

"Hit me with your best shot."

He lifted her legs and bent forward. The position left her knees nearly perpendicular with her shoulders and her pussy wide for his attention.

"I've noticed you like it hard." He kissed her, letting his lips and his words tickle her cheek.

"Mmm hmm."

"Hold on, Mrs. Young." He punctuated his warning with a quick, hard thrust and Riley groaned. He repeated the motion several more times, rejoicing when he felt the muscles of her pussy signaling her coming climax. Having sex with her was more fun than his fantasies had been. She far surpassed every wet dream he'd ever had about her.

He pulled out, releasing her legs.

"Hey." She frowned when he moved away.

"You're going to have to learn to control those orgasms of yours."

"Why?" she asked, and he laughed. The question was so typically Riley. She never denied herself any pleasure she wanted. Squeezing every bit of joy out of life she possibly could.

"Because it will make the reward that much sweeter in the end."

"Screw that. Actually, screw me. I was getting close."

"Haven't you ever heard the expression 'quality, not quantity'?"

"Has anyone ever told you that you talk too much in bed?"

He didn't bother to answer, instead rolling her onto her stomach and trapping her legs beneath his thighs. She started to push herself up, so he placed his hand at the top of her back, holding her against the mattress.

"Aaron, what—" Any further comment she could make was cut off when he placed a sharp smack on her bottom. "What the hell are you doing?"

He leaned forward, pressing his chest to her back. "Have you ever been spanked?"

"What kind of question is that? I'm one of seven rambunctious kids and you've met my pop. Of course I've been spanked. Hell, I think my pop spanked *you* once when we broke his—"

"I mean sexually, Riley."

"I don't think spankings are even remotely sexy."

"Have you ever tried it?" he asked.

"Have you?"

"Oh, hell yeah."

She laid her head on the pillow beneath her and sighed. "How did I not know all of this about you?"

He bent forward and placed a friendly kiss on her cheek before allowing her to roll over. He sat up while she lay on her back looking at him. "We've never really discussed our sex lives."

"That's not true," she said. "I've told you everything about mine."

He paused to consider her comment and realized she was being sincere. She'd told him way too much about her past love life, as far as he was concerned. It had eaten him alive to hear all the gory details about her being with any man who wasn't him. Even so, he'd listened and commented and pretended for years that every word she spoke didn't cut through him like a knife.

"You never asked me about mine, Riley."

"Would you have told me?" she asked. "If I'd looked at you and said, 'What floats your boat between the sheets, Aaron?' Would you have mentioned the spankings, the butt plugs, the dominance and God knows what else?"

Would he have told her? He wasn't sure he would have. For some reason, he'd wanted that part of his life to be separate from her. He hadn't lied earlier about wanting everything or nothing from her. Perhaps that was why he'd been so reticent in regards to telling her about his own sex life. Sharing even stories with Riley would have reminded him of what he wanted from her that he'd never expected—until yesterday—to receive.

"I wouldn't have told you," he confessed.

"Why not?" He could tell his answer hurt her. "We're best friends, Aaron. I honestly thought I knew everything there was to know about you."

"Would you have wanted to know all of this? Why does it matter? Until this morning, you've never viewed me as a man you'd want to fuck. I've always just been reliable old Aaron—your good buddy, your pal. You want to know what floats my boat between the sheets? I like to be in control in bed. If I tell a woman to get to her knees and suck my cock, I expect her to obey. If my lover is naughty, she can be damn sure I'll turn her over my knee and spank her ass. I like my pleasure with the slightest hint of pain. I love exploring all the unspeakable places on a woman's body and pushing her until she cries for mercy."

Riley stared at him for several long, painful moments, but he refused to break the silence. She'd pushed him and he'd pushed back. Gone were the days where he handled this woman with kid gloves. It was time she saw, time she understood what made him tick.

"I'd never cry for mercy." She rose up until her face was inches from his.

"What?"

"I'd only ever cry for more from you."

He blinked, trying to decide if he'd truly heard her or if he'd just imagined her response, until she continued.

"I'd be a liar and a fool if I pretended not to want

you. Just be warned, I'm not a woman who's commanded easily and if you ever try to do anything I don't want—"

"Riley, you don't even have to finish that sentence. You know better."

She nodded. "You're right. I do. So…you think spanking someone is sexy? Why?"

He grinned. "Do we want to do this show or tell style?"

She considered his request. "What if I'm not into pain?"

"Jesus, Riley. I'm not talking whips and chains and leather. Just my hand and your firm, sweet ass."

"Firm and sweet, huh? I thought you were a breast man."

He shook his head. "T-and-A man, all the way. I could never choose."

"What if I hate it?"

"I stop and we mark it off our list."

"We have a list?" She giggled at the thought.

He shrugged and tapped his head. "It's in here. We'll just have to find our way like any other married couple. I can promise you now, though, there's nothing you could refuse to do in bed that would break the deal. I'm married to you because I love you. Sex is only a part of our relationship."

She nodded. "Okay then. I guess we'll try the 'show' route. Do I get to return the favor one day?"

"You wanna spank my ass?" He wasn't surprised by her request. He knew deep inside their sex life would be one continual power struggle after another. There was a large part of him that looked forward to that challenge.

"I'd love to spank it," she confessed.

"We'll work up to it." He smiled as he spoke the words and she gave him a dirty look.

"I've noticed you say that a lot when you don't like the way the conversation is going."

He tapped his brow again. "It's all going on the list. I swear."

"Mmm hmm. Just so long as you remember," she imitated his tap on her own brow, "I have a very long memory."

He groaned. "Sadly, that is one thing I know about you all too well. Lay down on your stomach."

She looked confused for only a moment before she complied. "Don't you want me sprawled out facedown on your lap? Isn't the point to make you feel all powerful?"

"The point is to make *you* feel all hot and bothered, which is why I'd prefer it if you were sprawled out facedown next to me."

He lay down on his side with his head propped up by his left hand. With his right, he softly stroked her bare ass.

She hummed happily. "That feels nice."

He leaned down to kiss her forehead. "I always want to make you feel nice."

"You're doing a helluva good job so far, but aren't you sort of missing the point of this 'show, not tell' event?"

"You are the most impatient woman I've ever met."

She grinned. "Thank you."

He chuckled—and then brought his hand down against her rear end hard. She jerked and he could see he'd surprised her with his strength.

"Ouch." Her voice was low, rather than pained, but he knew his blow had definitely struck some nerves.

"No good?" He repeated the motion.

Her flinch was less visible this time and she didn't respond to the pain his action brought. "Is it supposed to be good?"

He spanked her three more times, his gaze never leaving her face where it rested on the pillow. He could see her struggling to accept his spankings.

"How does your ass feel?"

"Sore." She lifted her head and looked over her shoulder, down her back. "It's hot as fire. Are you leaving marks on it?"

"Hope so. Open your legs."

She hesitated.

"Trust me."

She shrugged and then spread her thighs. He rubbed one of her ass cheeks gently before moving his fingers to her pussy. He breathed a sigh of relief when he discovered the proof of her arousal. "You're wet."

"Seems to be my permanent state around you lately."

He smiled. "I like that."

"Figured you would."

He dipped one finger inside her passage and she groaned. He pulled out and then thrust inside her with two fingers several times before removing his hand and placing three more hard blows on various parts of her backside. She jumped in surprise and started to speak. He bent down to kiss her, quickly returning his fingers to her pussy. She moaned into his mouth as his lips claimed hers, as he savored the taste that was so uniquely Riley.

He repeated the same action several times until she was squirming against his fingers when they fucked her, raising her ass off the bed to meet his hard hand.

"Feel good?" He massaged her heated flesh. He looked down, enjoying the image of her ass marked by his hand.

"God, yes," she answered on a ragged breath.

He fought back the grin growing, certain Riley would misinterpret it. "What do you want, Riley?"

Her eyes, which had been closed, opened slowly to focus on him. "I want you inside me."

"Bend your knees, lift your ass in the air but keep your head down." She shivered slightly as he issued his command and he rewarded her obedience with a quick kiss on the cheek. "You're amazing."

"I'm horny as shit." She used the droll tone he loved so much. She might play his games, but she would never stop being herself.

"Guess I'd better see what I can do to take care of that."

"Seeing as how it's your fault."

She reached above her head, her palms lying flat against the headboard to support herself. She loved fast, hard fucks.

Lucky him. So did he.

He put just the head of his cock inside her, looking down to admire her body. Her ass was warm to the touch. He rubbed it, savoring the heat until she squirmed and tried to push against him.

He placed another smack on her bottom, a hard one, and she groaned. "You will wait for me, Riley."

"Dammit, Aaron." Her words were muffled, her face buried in the pillow.

He hit her again on the other ass cheek. "I'm sorry. Did you say something?"

She shuddered and he knew the effort it took for her to bite her tongue. He had no doubt once she'd gotten her orgasm, she would read him the riot act for acting like a superior ass. He smacked her again.

It would be worth it.

After several more blows, she gave him the one word he'd been waiting for.

"God, Aaron, *please*."

To hell with restraint. He wanted her—badly. He pushed in with one forceful thrust. She screamed and he felt the climax he'd denied her earlier start to return. She used her hands against the headboard, working in counter-rhythm to his motions, increasing the power of each incredible shove into her hot body.

She came, but he refused to acknowledge it. Refused to give up his personal heaven on earth so soon. Over and over he moved into her body, his grip on her hips tight as he pulled her toward him. Harder and harder. Faster and faster.

Her second climax came, stronger than the first, and he let it pull him into the vortex. "God, Riley." The words came out on a groan and she mimicked it with a moan of her own.

"Jesus, Aaron. You're going to kill me."

He pulled free of her body, only to help her flip onto her back. She trembled when he pushed his half erect cock back inside. He wasn't sure why, but he knew he wasn't ready to part from her yet. She sighed contentedly and stretched her arms above her head.

Resting his weight on his elbows, he took her face in his hands and kissed her softly. When they pulled apart, he pressed his forehead to hers, fighting back the grin trying to claw its way onto his face. His eyes must have given him away because she scowled at him.

"Cocky bastard."

"It was good, admit it." He kissed her again but didn't give her a chance to escape.

"It was tolerable." She shrugged noncommittally as she said the words but he wasn't fooled.

"It was awesome, Riley. The best."

"Don't get carried away, sugar."

"Say it, Mrs. Young. Say 'You just rocked my world, Aaron'."

She snorted with laughter. "If I say it, will you let me go to sleep, you lunatic."

"Only if you say it and mean it."

He was shocked to see her face—usually playful—sober up. "You rock my world, Aaron."

He immediately noticed she'd changed the tense of the verb. "I love you, Riley." She hadn't given the words back yet, but he wasn't worried. He knew she'd fight admitting that emotion harder than she would the marriage. He didn't mind. He knew her feelings even if she didn't, and he was nothing if not patient. He moved off her body, twisting her until they were spooning.

"Good night, Aaron."

"Night, angel."

She giggled softly and he could tell by the sound she'd be asleep within the next minute.

"What's so funny?" he whispered.

"I'm not an angel."

He tugged her closer and pressed a kiss on the back of her head. "You're *my* angel."

She sighed and he heard her breathing turn to the quiet, relaxed sound of sleep. He rubbed his face in her soft hair, following her into dreamland with a smile on this face.

CHAPTER SIX

Riley came awake with a start and tried to figure out what had roused her. She saw Aaron's silhouette sitting in a chair by the window, pulling on a sock.

"What's up?" she asked, rising. A glance at the clock showed her she'd slept less than an hour. "It's only midnight."

"I didn't mean to wake you. I'm going to head over to Jacko's bar, see if I can find Johnny Sparks."

Riley's tempered flared. "And you weren't going to wake me up?"

Aaron leaned back in the chair, and even in the dark room she could read the weariness in his posture. "I don't suppose I can ask you to sit this one out?"

She shook her head. "You're right. You can't."

"Riley, you heard Bubbles. Jacko's is a rough place."

"Which is exactly why I'm going. I'm not sending you into a place like that without backup."

He chuckled. "We may be in Vegas, but I'm not Grissom and you're not Catherine and this isn't *CSI*. Besides I'm a cop, I go into places like this all the time at home."

"Not without your partner." She had a valid point and she knew it. She rose as she spoke and began putting her discarded jeans back on.

"It's not safe and I *really* don't want you to go with me."

She paused in the process of pulling on her shirt. "Tough shit."

She finished tugging the shirt over her head. Her answer clearly annoyed him and she wondered how he would handle this argument. In the past, they'd often disagreed over her doing things he didn't approve of, but she'd always gotten her way because—as she pointed out—he had no say-so in what she did or where she went. Now that they were married, the rules had changed a bit. Though she had no intentions of letting him control her, she would have to take his concerns into account.

He stood and crossed the room. She stood up straighter, ready to do battle if needed. Though she understood he was afraid to take her into that bar, he failed to comprehend that she felt the same way about him. His job as a police officer had always bothered her, but she realized now exactly how difficult being married to a cop would be.

She tried to hide her discomfort at his silence. Arguments with Aaron were hell on her nerves. Damn man never worked on impulse, on emotion, like she did. He was a thinker and she could see him analyzing every flipping angle as they stared each other down.

"You're not going to win every argument, Riley."

"I know that."

He rubbed the back of his neck. "So you're gonna have to pick your battles. Decide which ones really matter to you. I know I've backed down in the past, but I'm not going to just lay down on every issue."

She reached out, placed her hands on his waist and took a step closer. "I don't expect you to. I just don't want you to go to that bar alone. Please don't ask me to stay here. I can't."

Her words seemed to take him aback and he studied her face too intently for her comfort. He cupped her cheek with one of his large palms and she tried not to melt under the gentle touch. "You'll stick to me like glue and you'll let me do all the talking. I don't ever want you more than five inches from me when we're in there. If you can't agree to that, I'll handcuff you to that bed to keep you here."

She smiled. "You kinky boy. You handcuff me to that bed and neither one of us will make it to that bar tonight."

"I'm serious, Riley."

"I won't leave your side and I won't say a word. Promise."

He shook his head. "Your pop and brothers would kick my ass if they knew I was planning to take you to a roughneck bar to question a pimp who could quite possibly have put a hit out on Trevor."

"I'll never tell." She ran her finger over her heart in

the shape of a cross and he blew out an exasperated breath.

"When we get back to Baltimore, we're going to have a long talk about my job."

She blinked twice, shocked by how well he knew her. "How did you know?"

He bent forward and kissed her forehead. "I know you."

She shook her head. "And yet you still married me. Crazy."

"Come on. The sooner we talk to the pimp, the sooner we can get back in bed. I'm getting damn sick and tired of having my honeymoon interrupted."

She grabbed her jacket and slid her cell phone in her back jeans pocket. "You're preaching to the choir, sugar."

JACKO'S WAS everything Bubbles described and more. Aaron suspected even Hell wouldn't welcome this establishment behind its gates. He tried to ignore the fact there appeared to be a drug deal going down in the parking lot. A guy was puking by the entrance as they walked up, clearly having met his limit of drinks two hours before he stopped drinking.

As they walked in the front door, he was assaulted by thick, rancid cigarette smoke and the twanging sound of country music blaring from a pair of speakers in the corner. A few tough-looking guys by the bar took his measure before he made it five steps inside, then their gazes landed on Riley and he could see the surprise on their faces. No man with half a brain in his head would bring a woman like Riley into a bar like this. For the hundredth time since they'd left the hotel, he wondered what the fuck he was doing.

It was her face as she'd looked at him, as she'd asked him not to leave her behind that had sealed the deal on his insanity. She was worried about him. Some foolish part of him had thought if he brought her along, let her see that he could handle himself in dives like this, she wouldn't worry as much when they returned to Baltimore and he returned to work. While that idea seemed a sound one in theory, the reality of bringing her to Jacko's was proving to be the most asinine thing he'd ever done in his life.

She tugged on his sleeve and pointed to the end of the bar. Through the haze of smoke and the crush of smelly bodies, she'd managed to spot Johnny. There was no missing him. Johnny Sparks was exactly as Bubbles had described and in the dim lighting, Aaron would swear he was looking at Wayne Newton in the flesh.

"Come on," he said. "Stay close."

He stepped up to the bar, catching the bartender's attention. He gestured for two beers, trying to decide where the safest spot for Riley was. If he put her in front of him, she'd be protected from all the men in the room, more than a few of whom were definitely checking her out. However, that would put her closest to Johnny. Deciding he could defend her against one rather than many more easily, he put her on the stool next to the pimp, while he stood behind her, pressing his chest against her back.

"Worry much?" she teased and he narrowed his eyes. One look at her face proved that while he was a nervous wreck, Riley was soaking up the atmosphere and already adapting. He reached over her shoulder for one of the beers the bartender delivered, trying to figure out the best way to engage Bella's pimp without tipping their hand too soon.

"You Johnny Sparks?" Riley asked, and Aaron fought back a groan.

The man narrowed his eyes before turning to look at them for the first time. Aaron spotted the same surprise on Johnny's face as he'd seen on the other customers in the bar when he saw tiny, clean-cut, pretty Riley sitting next to him. One quick glance around the bar confirmed that the only women who frequented the joint were either hardened hookers or tattooed amazons who could hold their own.

"Who wants to know?" he asked and Aaron gripped Riley's waist, warning her that he was supposed to be questioning the man.

"I do," she said, her tone pure smartass.

Johnny didn't seem to know how to respond. "Who the hell are you?"

"Riley Collins…er, Young." She put her hand out for a handshake and again, her actions seemed to fluster the man. He reached out and accepted her hand. "Nice to meet you. We're friends of Bella's."

"Riley," Aaron muttered. "I thought I was going to handle this."

"You know Bella?" Johnny asked. "You seen her lately?"

Riley shook her head. "I don't really remember ever seeing her, but apparently I met her last night. Unfortunately I was sort of trashed."

It appeared trashed was a state Johnny could relate to and understand. "You don't happen to remember seeing her with some big shot gambler from out of town, do you?"

Riley snorted. "Big shot gambler? Trev?"

Aaron tightened his grip. He'd lost control of this situation in less than five minutes. Johnny's eyes narrowed when she mentioned Trevor's name.

"Trev?" Johnny asked. "Is that the motherfucker's name?" His tone had crossed from bored to pure, pulsating anger. "You know him?" His eyes narrowed and he leaned closer. Suddenly Aaron was regretting putting Riley in front of him.

"Listen, Johnny—" he began quickly, trying to divert the man's attention from his newlywed wife.

"Shut the fuck up," Johnny said menacingly. "I'm talking to the woman."

Aaron felt Riley's back stiffen. "Don't you talk to my husband that way."

Johnny's face darkened with fury. "Listen you little whore, if you know where my Bella is, you better start talking *now*."

Riley attempted to lean toward the furious man but Aaron held her back. Jesus, now he had two pissed-off loose cannons to deal with. Yeah, coming here had *not* been a fantastic idea and he could see Tris taking a swing at him if he ever found out.

"Let's go, Riley," he said, leaning down to speak in her ear to be heard over the loud music. "He doesn't know where she is. This is a lost cause and I think we've overstayed our welcome." A quick survey of the room proved a couple of men were getting brave as they started to move closer. In about two minutes, he suspected things were going to get very ugly.

Riley shrugged off his hand as he tried to pull her off the barstool. "Did you call me a whore?" Riley asked.

"Tell me where Bella is." Johnny stood, his voice raised over the din in the room. The two men who had been approaching them took one look at Johnny and turned around. Great, Aaron thought. The regulars were afraid of the pissed-off Wayne Newton wannabe. This wasn't good.

"Or what?" Riley taunted. "You gonna order up a hit on me too?"

Aaron closed his eyes briefly and prayed for the patience not to turn Riley over his lap right here and spank her ass for real. "That's it. We're fucking leaving."

"A hit?" Johnny seemed completely taken off-guard by her comment.

"A friend of ours said you ordered a hit on the last guy Bella took off with." Aaron shook his head. Jesus, Riley sucked at the subtle art of interrogation. She'd just blazed her way across the bar and asked what she wanted to know. His first instinct was to pick her up, throw her over his shoulder and get her the hell out of there.

Johnny's response, however, pulled him up short.

"A hit?" Johnny repeated, this time roaring with laughter as he said it. Aaron looked around and noticed the room full of drunks almost seemed to release a sigh of relief. He wished he felt as comforted. "Holy fuck. That is so twisted and stupid, it's funny. How the hell could I order up a hit? And what dumb cunt told you that?"

Riley looked back at him and gestured as if to say, "*He* gets to use that word", and Aaron narrowed his gaze. "What happened to letting me handle this?"

"You take too long. Hell, we'd still be sitting here sipping our beers if I'd left it up to you. I'm sort of horny. It *is* my honeymoon, remember?"

Aaron shook his head. "This is my job, Riley. There's nothing wrong with erring on the side of caution. Taking your time to feel out the situation."

She rolled her eyes at him. "Jaysus. I can tell you right now, I'm not gonna spend my life waiting around for you to make decisions. I do *not* have time for that shit."

"Listen, sweetheart…" He dragged out the term of endearment, lacing it with as much sarcasm as he could muster. "All I'm saying is—"

"Who the hell *are* you two?" Johnny's laughter had subsided, but at least his anger hadn't returned. Aaron began to get a sense the man wasn't as dangerous as they'd been led to believe. Despite his odd attire, he looked as though he could just as easily be sitting at the end of the bar in Pat's Pub, shooting the shit over the latest sporting event with Riley's pop and brothers.

Riley turned and gave Johnny an exasperated look. "I told you. I'm Riley Young. This conversation is going to take too damn long if I have to keep repeating myself. Your…" She paused and Aaron assumed she was searching for a polite word for prostitute. "Lady friend, Bella, was last seen with our friend Trev. Trev's wife is here now and she's looking for him. We said we'd help because she's just found out she's pregnant." After a brief pause, she added, "With Trev's baby. We were hoping you might know where he and Bella are. Maybe you could help us find them."

Johnny shrugged. "And why should I try to help you find this man for his knocked-up wife?"

"You do *not* want a pissed-off, hormone-imbalanced Johanna Blankenship running around Vegas. She makes this room of roughnecks look like a bunch of choir boys."

For the first time since they'd engaged the man in conversation, Johnny's gaze landed on him. "You married this woman?"

Aaron nodded wearily.

"Voluntarily?"

Aaron barked out a brief laugh as Riley put her hands on her hips. "Oh, that's rich. You're sitting here dressed like a washed-up goddamn Vegas singer and you're criticizing my husband's choice for a wife?"

"Wayne Newton is far from washed up!" Aaron could see Johnny's previous anger was nothing in comparison to his sudden fury now. Obviously, Riley had attacked him on a very personal level. "Where the fuck are you from? Wayne Newton has performed over thirty thousand shows here in Vegas—at the Tropicana, the Stardust. He has a street named after him. He was on *Dancing with the goddamn fucking Stars*. Jesus, they call him Mr. Las Vegas, for fuck sake! Where's your respect?" His voice and his body had risen throughout his recitation of Wayne's resume until he was towering over them, and quite a few of the people sitting nearby moved away.

The bartender stepped closer and looked at Aaron. "Did you just insult Wayne Newton in front of Johnny?"

Aaron shook his head.

Johnny pointed at Riley. "No. She did."

"They call him Mr. Las Vegas?" she asked. "Seriously?"

Shaking his head, Johnny resumed his seat on his barstool. "Fucking tourists. Yes. That's what they call him."

"Well, that's pretty cool. Sorry I called him washed-up."

Johnny just stared at her and Aaron sort of felt a bit of sympathy for the man. Riley could wear out the most patient of souls. "I don't know where your friend is. I wish I did. Bella—" Johnny's voice cracked on the woman's name and Aaron realized they'd found the chink in the man's armor.

"You love her." Her words weren't a question, but a simple statement.

Johnny nodded. "Course I do. Been asking her to marry me for months now."

Aaron felt the same confusion he saw written on Riley's face. However, while *he* figured out they'd misinterpreted the information Bubbles gave them, Riley didn't make the leap as quickly.

"Wow. Never heard of a pimp marrying one of his girls."

Aaron groaned and feared her comment would set Johnny off again. He tried to divert the disaster. "Um, Riley. I don't think—"

"Pimp?" Johnny asked. His body shook with laughter and for several minutes, they could only sit and wait as the man struggled to regain his composure. Each time Aaron thought he'd pulled himself together, he'd begin wheezing with laughter that turned into a coughing fit that ended once again with laughter. His face was purple with merriment and there were tears streaming down his face.

Riley looked back at Aaron. "I think maybe we jumped to the wrong conclusion after talking to Bubbles."

"What was your first clue?"

"I've sort of fucked this all up, haven't I?"

Aaron shrugged. They weren't dead. They hadn't been robbed. Johnny wasn't the mob-connected pimp they'd feared. Really, the only bad part of this little excursion was they still didn't have a clue where Trev was. "Yeah, you did, and yet, in typical Riley fashion, you appear to have emerged unscathed."

"Sorry we bothered you, Johnny," she said, starting

to rise. Discovering they were leaving, Johnny sobered up, his peals of laughter dying down.

"Where you going? The night's still young. Let me buy you two a drink and you can tell me where you got the fool notion I was a pimp." Speaking the word *pimp* caused Johnny to chuckle once more.

"That's okay," Aaron started, but Riley resumed her seat as Johnny waved the bartender over.

Fuck. They'd been so close to escaping.

"I think we just sort of misinterpreted something our friend Bubbles said," Riley explained.

"Sounds to me like you misheard everything that stupid cow said. What makes you think I can put a hit out on somebody?"

The bartender brought another round of beers and Aaron pulled an empty stool over, placing it right up against Riley's. She gave him a look that told him to back off, but he ignored it. Despite the fact Johnny appeared to be harmless, that didn't mean the other men in the bar were.

"Bubbles said the last time Bella ran off with a guy, you put a hit on him."

Johnny grinned and Aaron was taken aback by how much the guy really did look like Wayne Newton. In this dim lighting, hidden behind the haze of cigarette smoke, he was actually a dead ringer.

"Bella didn't run off with that guy and I didn't *put* a hit on him. I *hit* him. With my cab."

"Cab?" Riley asked.

"I'm a taxi driver, not a pimp."

"And you hit a guy with your car?"

Johnny shrugged. "It's not like I killed him or anything. Fucker was climbing out of our bedroom window—mine and Bella's. Guess they'd heard my car pull up to the curb. Caught a glimpse of him coming out of the house and I gunned the engine. Chased the prick for two blocks before I was able to clip him from behind and knock him down. Got out of the cab, beat the shit outta him and then went home. That's it."

Aaron was suddenly grateful for his job on the force in Baltimore. Though Maryland had its fair share of crazies, Vegas seemed to hold the current record.

"Good for you." Riley raised her glass to toast Johnny.

Aaron looked at her with disbelief. "Good for him? Riley, he chased the guy down with his car."

"The guy was screwing his girlfriend. In Johnny's house. Hell, in Johnny's *bed*."

Johnny nodded, clearly delighted that Riley was defending him. "I had to flip the mattress. Couldn't get the image of that fucker rutting away in my spot out of my mind."

Riley gestured to Johnny as if his comments reiterated what she'd just said. Aaron started to restate his stance, but the determined looks on Riley's and Johnny's faces proved anything else he said would be a waste of breath. He tried not to dwell on the fact that his wife's opinions of right and wrong aligned more closely with the Wayne Newton taxi driver's than his. Oh yeah, the next fifty years or so were going to be very interesting.

Riley reached over and patted the man's hand

sympathetically. "You know, Johnny, I hate to bring up a sore subject, but Bella doesn't seem to be the most faithful of girlfriends. Are you sure you might not be better off without her?"

Riley's comforting touch and softly spoken words seemed to open the floodgates and for the second time in one day, they watched a person fall apart due to Trev and Bella's desertion.

"It's not Bella's fault," he blubbered. "It's mine. I've been putting too much pressure on her. She was bound to break under the stress."

"Pressure?" Riley asked.

"I want to get married, start a family, but Bella's focused on her career. Claims having a baby would ruin that."

It just dawned on Aaron that he didn't know what Bella did, now that hooker had been crossed off the list. "Her career?"

Johnny looked at him. "She's a stripper. Best fucking stripper in Vegas."

"Ah." Riley nodded with understanding. "I guess having a baby could interfere with that."

"My Bella's not a bad girl. It's just she has these needs."

Aaron recalled the clerk at Sal's talking about Bella's penchant for pony play. He took a long swig of beer, hoping to finish it quickly and move on. The last thing he needed was for Riley's curiosity to be piqued over that particular sex kink. He had absolutely no interest in putting a bit in Riley's mouth and riding her around the bedroom.

"Needs?" Riley prompted.

Aaron looked at his watch. "Um, Riley. It's getting kind of late," he murmured in her ear. She gave him a look like he was a heartless bastard for suggesting they leave Johnny while he was so upset.

Johnny didn't seem to notice their exchange as he began pouring out all his woes.

Aaron waved the bartender over and ordered another beer. Might as well get comfortable. He knew Riley wouldn't leave until she'd heard every sordid and twisted tale Johnny Sparks had to share. He'd spent many a night like this, sitting at a bar as Riley served as counselor to every misfit toy on the island.

Johnny explained Bella's fascination and need to be in the spotlight. "She was born to be a star. Born to be admired. She gets up on that stage and I swear to God, it's like magic."

"But that doesn't explain why she feels the need to cheat on you, Johnny. You know, you really shouldn't put up with that shit. If Aaron ever cheated on me, I'd cut his dick off."

Aaron looked at her with a playful grin, tapping his brow. "I'm definitely filing that useful piece of information away for future reference."

Riley gave him an annoyed glance. "You'd never cheat on me."

"You're right. I wouldn't. Although it *is* my honeymoon and we *have* been in this bar a long time…"

She gave him a breathtaking grin. "I'll make it up to you. Later."

He scowled as she turned back to Johnny. "If you're

really in love with Bella, you need to put your foot down. Tell her it's you or the highway and you're gonna have to tell her no more affairs."

Johnny looked down miserably. "I wish I could, but what do I have to offer her? I'm lucky the woman looked my way to begin with. What do I have to hold a woman like her?"

It was clear the man worshiped the ground his unfaithful girlfriend walked on. Aaron sort of felt sorry for the guy.

"Are you kidding me? You're a good-looking guy. You've got your own business. I mean, it's your taxi, right?"

Johnny nodded. "Yeah. I'm an independent businessman."

Just not a successful one, Aaron thought. He figured that explained why Johnny was able to close down Jacko's every night rather than work.

Riley rested her cheek on her hand. "You know, Johnny. I've been wondering. How come you don't do impersonation work? You've got this Wayne Newton look down pat."

"I can't sing."

"What?" Aaron asked.

"I'm tone deaf. Can't sing a note."

Aaron rubbed his face wearily and wondered how he got here. Two days ago he'd been hanging out in his own apartment in Baltimore, minding his own business and watching baseball on the television. One phone call from Keira later, he was all the way across the country, sitting in a Vegas dive with a tone deaf Wayne

Newton look-alike, looking for Trev and a stripper and to top it all off, he was now married to Riley Collins.

Glancing over at his new wife, he grinned. Aside from the fact he was in Vegas, this night with her wasn't all that different than a thousand other nights he'd spent in her presence. The woman had a knack for finding trouble and still landing on her feet.

"Wow," he heard her say, "that sucks. But do you have to be able to sing? Can't you just lip-synch?"

Johnny shrugged. "It's not just the singing. I, um…" He lowered his voice and Aaron found himself leaning closer to hear his next words. "I've got terrible stage fright. Can't get up in front of people without shitting in my pants."

"Oh." Riley turned to face Aaron and mouthed the letters *TMI*. He fought back a grin at her joke as she twisted back to Johnny. "Listen, Johnny," she said, grabbing a fresh napkin and asking the bartender for a pen. "This is my cell phone number. If Bella should come home, would you call me? We're really pretty anxious to find Trev."

Johnny's face darkened as she said Trevor's name. "Oh, I'll call you," he assured her. "Right after I plow the fucker over with my cab."

Riley sighed. "Truth be told, Johnny, I think your plans for Trev might be kinder than his wife's when she finds out he cheated on her."

Johnny perked up at her comment. "Really?"
She nodded.
"Then I'll make sure not to kill him with my cab.

Want to make sure he's alive to get the wife's treatment too."

Riley laughed. "You're a heartless bastard, Johnny."

He smiled at her. "And you're not so bad for a tourist, Riley. Even if you do know fuck-all about Wayne Newton."

Aaron added his goodbyes to the mix and tugged Riley out of the bar. He'd never been so happy to be outside in the fresh, clean air.

"Ew," Riley said, scrunching up her nose. "We stink."

"Stale smoke and beer. What do you say we go back to the hotel and take a shower together? I'll even let you suck my cock."

She laughed. "Gee thanks, sugar. Actually that doesn't sound like such a bad plan. The shower part," she clarified.

"Hey, you're the one who promised to make up the fact we just spent an hour longer in that dive than we needed to."

"Johnny was distraught. We couldn't leave him like that."

Aaron sort of thought they could. The man had been three sheets to the wind and he wasn't sure Johnny was even going to remember talking to them come morning.

"There you two are!" a loud voice said from behind them.

Aaron turned, surprised to find Bubbles jiggling her way across the parking lot toward them. He wondered if she realized her spandex top really wasn't a suitable replacement for a bra.

"Hey, Bubbles. What are you doing here?" Riley asked.

"I figured you guys would come looking for Johnny. I've been waiting out here almost an hour. I was just about to give up. Time is money, you know. Thought maybe you'd chickened out. Were you in there that whole time?"

Riley nodded and Aaron saw the hooker was impressed. "Dayum, *chica*. You're a crazier bitch than me."

Aaron tried to ignore the fact Riley took Bubbles' comment as a compliment.

"Was there a reason you were looking for us, Bubbles?" he asked, not forgetting the promise of a shower and possibly a blowjob looming in his very near future.

"Did Johnny know where Bella was?"

Riley shook her head. "Nope. And he's not happy."

"Didn't figure he would be after the hit he put on that last guy. Put the poor guy in the hospital for nearly a week. Johnny may be stupid as pigeon shit, but he's strong and mean when riled."

Aaron had to agree with that assessment.

"Anyway, I was thinking after you left. Maybe you should go to Swingers."

"Swingers?" Aaron asked.

"It's the strip club where Bella works. Fucking bitch stole the job I wanted."

"You wanted to be a stripper?" Riley's voice expressed her surprise.

"Are you fucking kidding me? Who *wouldn't* want to be a stripper? All that money, men looking but not really touching. It's a dream job. Way better than being a fucking ho."

"So why are you a hooker if you hate it? You're a smart woman, pretty face. I'm sure you could find lots of jobs."

Bubbles shrugged. "Not as easy as you think. Sort of fell into the hooking after high school, got into some money troubles and sex was a quick way to make a buck. Now people know me around here. I got a reputation. Ain't nobody gonna hire a hooker for any respectable job."

"So move somewhere else," Riley suggested.

"With what? Monopoly money? Besides, where would I go? I was born in Vegas. Only place I've ever been. I got friends here."

Riley fell silent and Aaron tried to beat back his sixth sense that said her sudden quietness couldn't be good. Anxious to distract her from whatever plot she was cooking up, he latched onto the first thing that popped into his mind.

"So where is this Swingers?" he asked.

Riley glanced at him, a smile crossing her face. "You wanna go to the strip club?"

"Why not? For all we know, she's taking a spin on the pole as we speak. Johnny mentioned her love of the spotlight. And if not, maybe Bella called in and quit.

Maybe she told her boss where she was going. It's worth a shot, I suppose."

Bubbles hitched her oversized tote bag on her shoulder and fluffed up her already voluminous pink hair. "You two mind if I tag along? Figure if Bella cut and run, the boss might finally give me a shot at her spot."

"Sure. The more, the merrier," Riley said. "You can tell us how to get there."

Riley and Bubbles headed off toward the corner in search of a cab, chatting away as if they'd been friends forever. He fell into step behind them and listened as Riley espoused about the wonders of Baltimore.

Fuck. It sounded like his wife was trying to talk Bubbles into considering a move to the east coast if the stripping job didn't pan out.

The images of her pop's face and those of Riley's four brothers crossed his mind. Riley was infamous for bringing home strays—injured pigeons, dogs, once she even found and rescued a blind rat. Hell, just a couple weeks ago, she'd started putting milk out on the back stoop of the restaurant for a small kitten she'd found.

Bubbles laughed loudly at something Riley said and Aaron sighed. Yep. He could see it now. Bubbles was the ultimate stray.

CHAPTER SEVEN

Riley laughed as they entered Swingers. While Aaron was a pretty worldly guy—his job as a cop ensured that he'd seen plenty—she couldn't miss the slight blush that stained his cheeks when they were led to a table by the almost naked, bald hostess. Totally bald. There wasn't a hair anywhere on the woman—a truth driven home by the fact she was basically wearing two strings, one around her waist and one between her legs. Riley assumed this was her version of a thong. Her husband's eyebrows rose to his hairline when he first spotted her, but in typical Aaron fashion, he recovered quickly.

"That was interesting," he said after she took their drink orders and left. It was nearly two a.m. and the place was in full swing. There were two women performing. One was dressed in a skimpy police outfit —her badge attached to her naked breast through a nipple piercing. She was swinging a billy club as a blonde woman she'd handcuffed to the pole gyrated and pretended to resist arrest. As she moved, her clothing began to fall away, piece by piece, until she was left in just a thong.

The crowd—equal parts male and female—was urging the policewoman to use her billy club on her captive. She began rubbing it between the other woman's legs to great applause.

"Damn. This is a strip club?" Riley asked.

Bubbles shrugged. "Swingers sort of blurs the line. It's connected to Swingers Too through those doors over there. That's a full-fledged sex club. This is just sort of the warm-up. The girls get the customers so hot and bothered they'll drop the hundred-buck cover charge for Swingers Too without blinking an eye."

Riley watched a couple hand over a wad of bills and pass through the door to the other club. Good business sense, she decided.

As that show ended, two more women came onstage to act out the roles of teacher and naughty schoolgirl. Riley squeezed her legs together and tried to ignore Aaron's smug glances when the teacher used a ruler on the student's ass as punishment.

"Looks like fun," he murmured to her. "List worthy?"

She wanted to smack him for his cockiness, but instead her traitorous body forced her to merely nod. His genuinely pleased grin prompted her to respond with one of her own. "I had no idea you were such a dirty boy."

He wiggled his eyebrows suggestively. "You have no

idea *how* dirty." He dragged his hand down her arm, moving inward very discreetly to pinch one of her turgid nipples. She gasped as his quick squeeze sent a jolt of arousal straight to her aching clit.

She leaned closer to him. "I'm horny."

Aaron's smoldering gaze let her know he was sharing her pain. "Let's see if we can find the manager and ask about Bella." He glanced at his watch. "I have every intention of having you naked, your ass filled with that butt plug and chained to the hotel bed while I fuck you raw within the hour."

Riley swallowed heavily, her panties soaked with the sticky juices his sexy promise produced. "Make that within half an hour," she said, her voice huskily betraying her need.

He nodded. "Deal."

Bubbles followed them as they stood and walked to the bar. The woman was hell-bent on trying to get a job at the club. While Riley appreciated the fact she wanted to give up prostituting herself, she wished Bubbles would branch out to an entirely different line of work. Maybe one that let her remain dressed.

Aaron asked the bartender about the manager and the man directed them to a small door near the restrooms. They knocked on the door and were bid to enter. The manager was seated behind the desk and Riley was shocked by his appearance. She'd antici-pated a swarthy guy who walked with a swagger and wore his shirt unbuttoned to show off all his bling. This man looked like her sister-in-law Lily's dad, the straight-laced government employee. The manager was a short, slight man with reading glasses and a bad comb-over.

Aaron introduced himself and briefly explained why they were looking for Bella. Riley was getting bored with the story simply because of the number of times they'd been forced to retell it.

The manager, Louis, nodded as Aaron finished his recitation.

"She called in and quit."

"When?" Aaron asked.

"Late last night. Saturday's her night off anyway. Tonight's a different story. I'm totally pissed off. There was no way I could find a pony girl in one day. She's my main act." Louis glanced at the clock on his wall. "In about thirty minutes, I'm going to have to take that stage and tell those horny drunks that the star attraction isn't here." Louis picked up a glass of milky-looking water from his desk and chugged it down. Riley figured he was dosing himself on a little plop, plop, fizz, fizz. "My fucking gut is killing me too. Do you know what this is gonna do to business until I can find a damn replacement?"

"I can be your pony girl." Bubbles had been remarkably quiet the entire time they were in the office, standing by the door. For a moment, Riley had forgotten about her. An amazing feat, considering Bubbles was pretty hard to ignore.

Louis looked up and grimaced. He obviously hadn't been aware of her presence either. "Jesus, Bubbles. Are we gonna have to go through this again? You know I'm not gonna let you be the pony girl."

"Why not?" Riley asked. Regardless of Bubbles' rather outlandish outfits, she couldn't help but think the crowd she'd just been a part of would love seeing Bubbles' girls.

Louis rolled his eyes. "Why not? I'll tell you why not. Because she can't dance. Woman has two left feet."

"But I been practicing," Bubbles insisted.

Louis snorted with impatience. "You said that last time and you fell off the stage and broke a table. Why don't you just accept the fact that not everybody's cut out to be a stripper and you happen to be in that group?"

"But I'm just saying, if you'll give me another chance, let the crowd see me. I know they'd—"

"You want me to put you onstage *tonight*? In front of witnesses? Jesus, you'd hurt somebody."

"Surely you have women working here who aren't onstage. What about a hostess job? Or a lap-dance lady?" Riley suggested.

"I don't need any hostesses and the performers do the lap dances too. There's no distinction."

Riley walked over, taking Bubbles' hand and dragging her closer to Louis. His lack of height put him almost at eye level with the hooker's most profitable asset. "But Bubbles could be your *special* lap-dance lady. Do you know how much money men would pay to have these beauties thrust in their face?"

The manager's face took on a greedy, thoughtful look.

"How much would *you* pay, Aaron?" Riley prompted, throwing him an *answer right or pay later* look.

"Oh damn," Aaron said. "At least fifty." Riley's eyes narrowed. "A hundred dollars. I'd slap down a hundred bucks without even giving it a second thought."

"Really?" Louis asked.

Riley got a sense she was close to victory, but Louis didn't concede as easily as she'd hoped.

"She still can't dance. Even lap dances require a bit of rhythm. She has none."

"I'll teach her."

From the corner of her eye, she saw Aaron's head jerk toward her. "What?"

Riley looked at her husband. "I'm going to teach Bubbles how to give the world's greatest lap dance. You have an empty room?"

She thought she heard Aaron mutter "Jesus" but she wasn't sure if it was said as a curse or a prayer.

"You can use my office," Louis offered. "You've got fifteen minutes, at which time I'm coming back. If she doesn't give me the sexiest lap dance on earth then she has to promise me she'll never come back here looking for a job again. Deal?"

Riley wasn't completely satisfied with the bargain. "If she *does* give you a great lap dance, you hire her and make her your main attraction and give her," Riley paused, wondering what the split was for exotic dancers, "fifty percent of her take."

Louis laughed and shook his head. "I'll give her thirty percent."

Riley opened her mouth to dicker some more. She loved squeezing blood from a turnip, but damn Bubbles yelled out "Deal!" before she could demand forty.

"If she manages to get me off, I'll introduce her tonight. Might distract the wolves enough that they won't mind Bella's absence. Fifteen minutes."

Louis closed the door behind him and Riley walked behind the desk, pulling his chair around to the middle of the room. "We're going to need some room to move." Glancing around, she found an iPod docked with some small speakers. "Perfect. Bubbles, you try to find a sexy song on Louis' play list and Aaron, you sit here."

He dug in his heels, refusing to move. "Me?"

Riley gestured at the chair, annoyed by his reticence. "Um, hello? Lap dance. We sort of need a lap."

"You're going to have Bubbles give me a lap dance?"

"Oh for God's sake, Aaron. I'm going to show her how first and then I thought she could try out a few moves. It's not like I'm hiring you a prostitute. I'm teaching her how to dance."

"And what makes you an expert on lap dances?"

She rolled her eyes, impatient with his stalling. "I took that pole-dancing class at the community center a couple years ago, remember? We've only got fifteen minutes. Sit down."

Aaron sat on the chair with a scowl. "You're gonna owe me for this, Riley. Big time."

"Fine," she replied hastily. "I'll give you a *get off however you want* card. Now hush."

Bubbles pushed play and the sultry sounds of a jazz tune filled the air. Riley indicated that Bubbles should stand behind Aaron, but slightly to the right so she would be able to see everything clearly.

Swaying her hips, Riley let the music filter through her body as she moved closer to him.

AARON SWALLOWED HEAVILY when Riley's arm brushed up against his. His cock had gone on full alert the second she told him to sit down. There was no way he was going to be able to withstand Riley giving him a sexy lap dance for fifteen whole minutes. He'd been seconds away from dragging her into Swingers Too after her face flushed with excitement when the stripper took the ruler to the other woman's ass.

He couldn't hold back a groan when Riley threw one leg over his lap, her body swaying and hovering over his. God, she was amazing. Throughout her dance she spoke softly to Bubbles, giving her directions, advice, but the words couldn't penetrate Aaron's lust-filled mind. All he could see, all he could feel was Riley's body as it gyrated, tantalizing him with the need for more.

He raised his hands to engulf her waist, to pull her down on his covered cock. He felt like a randy boy, ready and willing to settle for a dry hump if that was all she'd allow. He'd beg for it too.

She smacked his hands away. "You can look, but no touching."

He reached down and placed his hands on the seat of the chair, tightening his grip, certain there was no way he could keep his hands away from her generous, perky breasts. She was cupping them from underneath, pushing them up and leaning forward until he thought for a moment he'd felt her nipple brush his chin.

He licked his lips, fighting the impulse to move toward her, to capture that juicy nipple with his teeth. Every motion of her body screamed sex and he was reminded of the image of her in the throes of orgasm earlier in the night.

"Please, Riley…enough," he murmured, his knuckles white with the effort of not touching her. She looked at his face, her hand caressing his cheek. Smiling sweetly, she lowered herself, the vee of her legs perfectly aligned against his erection. She rubbed deeply enough that the heat of her pussy reached his cock through the denim of his jeans. Fuck. He had no doubt if she continued, he'd come in his pants.

"You want me," she whispered in his ear, her teeth biting his earlobe.

His breathing was harsh, his lungs expanding and contracting at too fast a pace as he tried to fight down the part of him that was about to give Bubbles an education in a lap dance gone too far.

"You're about to get fucked, Mrs. Young. There *is* such a thing as teasing a man beyond his breaking point."

His words seemed to soak in and he realized she'd been as swept away by desire as he was.

"Shit," she muttered. She blinked quickly and tried to compose herself. Hell, he thought she'd been teasing, but it was obvious she'd been as turned-on as he was. He grinned. He was a lucky man. His new wife had one helluva libido and he was going to make sure she never geared down out of overdrive.

"That was so hot," Bubbles said, reminding them both that they had a witness. Aaron grimaced with pain as Riley stood up and stepped away. How the hell was he supposed to get back to the hotel with a hard-on?

"So…" Riley cleared her throat. "The idea is to just sway. The beauty of the lap dance is you don't have to be a great dancer to achieve it. Just use those, um, gifts God gave you and have fun."

Bubbles approached and for a moment, he feared Riley was still going to let the hooker try out a few of those suggested moves on him. He was a second away from blowing his load. A strong wind would send him over the edge, but he wasn't sure his new wife would understand him coming in his pants while another woman danced around him.

"Um, Riley," he started, but she winked.

"I think you're going to have to fly solo for the first time with Louis. Aaron and I really, *really* need to head back to the hotel. I'm sort of tired."

Bubbles laughed, clearly not fooled by Riley's sudden need for sleep. "I'm sure you are, *chica*. Looks to me like this man could keep a girl tired for a lifetime."

Riley laughed as he rose slowly. His cock was still stiff as a pike so he pulled his untucked shirt lower and prayed it would be enough to cover him on the street. He figured every guy in the bar was sporting a woody, so it wouldn't be a big deal until they left Lustville and rejoined the land of the gamblers.

"Break a leg, Bubbles. I really hope—"

A knock on the door interrupted Riley's comments and Louis walked back in. "Time's up. You ready, Bubbles?"

Bubbles nodded and waved as they left the office.

The cab ride back to the hotel seemed to last an eternity. Looking out the window, Aaron never ceased to be amazed by the crowds on the streets. It was pushing three a.m. and the sidewalks were still abuzz with activity.

As they entered the hotel room, he pushed Riley back against the door.

"Again?" she teased. "You're gonna have to find a new move, sugar."

"Take off your clothes." He'd already pulled his T-shirt over his head and was working his jeans over his hips as he spoke. She followed suit and he was impressed to see she could strip down to total nakedness in less than sixty seconds.

"Very good," he murmured when the last piece of clothing, her bra, hit the floor. There were no preliminaries, no foreplay as he grasped her ass, lifted her and impaled himself to the hilt in one hard thrust. Riley threw her head back against the door as she wrapped her legs around his waist and met his pummeling with some hard thrusts of her own. Obviously, the dance had triggered powerful needs in her as well.

"Harder," she cried and Aaron doubled his efforts, moved into her until he felt lightheaded from the fact all the blood in his body appeared to have defected to his cock.

"God," she yelled. "Yes, yes!" She came in a rush,

her pussy muscles pumping hard against him, clenching him tighter than he'd ever dared to grip himself in masturbation. He forced his way deeper and felt her come again. His balls filled, the come exploding from the tip of his cock almost painfully. When the last drop fell, he withdrew and slowly went to his knees, her back sliding against the door until her ass reached the floor.

"Holy shit," he mumbled. "That was so fucking good." He kissed her then. Kissed her hard, kissed her soft. Long kisses and short ones. All he knew was he wanted the air he breathed to be hers.

"I love you, Riley. I love you so much."

"Aaron," she whispered. He opened his eyes, looked into hers and found his response. She was as overwhelmed by the power of the moment as he was.

Pressing his lips to hers once more, he drank her answer down in a flurry of deep, wet, sweeter-than-chocolate kisses. When they finally parted, she smiled almost shyly—the one personality trait he'd never seen in her. It passed quickly.

"I think my ass fell asleep." Her words were light, fun, thoroughly her.

He rose and reached down to help her up. "Well, we can't have that. What do you say we try to wake it up with a nice hot shower?"

"Sounds like a plan."

"And then you and I are going to get serious about this honeymoon."

She laughed as they walked to the bathroom. "That wasn't serious?"

He pinched her ass as she bent over to turn on the

water and she squealed. "You ain't seen nothing yet, Riley Young."

She turned to look at him. "I like the sound of that, you know."

"The promise of more sex?"

She shook her head. "Riley Young. It should feel weird, but for some reason—"

"It fits," he finished for her.

She nodded. "*We* fit."

He grinned and placed a quick kiss on her forehead. "We've always fit, Riley. Just took you awhile to wise up to that fact."

She turned back to the shower to check the water before glancing over her shoulder and giving him a mischievous smile. "To wise up or to resign myself to it?"

He slapped her ass as she stepped into the stall.

"Hey," she protested.

"You said it was asleep. I just thought I'd wake it up for you."

She reached out and grasped his half-hard cock in her hand. He groaned.

"I can think of much more fun things to wake up." She dropped to her knees as she spoke and Aaron decided she had a point. An excellent point.

CHAPTER EIGHT

A s they emerged from the bathroom, wrapped in
towels, Riley looked at the clock and decided
she'd finally found a city that understood her hours.
Always a night owl, she loved the hustle and bustle the
Vegas nights offered.

"I feel like I lived a lifetime in one day."

Aaron walked up behind her and wrapped his arms
around her waist, tugging her towel off as he did so. "It
was a pretty eventful day. Leaves me to wonder what
tomorrow will bring."

"I think it *is* tomorrow," she teased.

His hands drifted up to cup her breasts, pulling her
back against his chest and holding her there tightly. She
wiggled her ass, trying to entice his cock to come out to
play once more. After a quick blowjob, they'd decided
to forego the shower and instead filled up the bathtub,
soaking and talking for nearly an hour.

Plenty of recovery time for her newfound toy. She

started to reach down to grip him but he swatted her hands away.

"I want to play," she said, reaching for his dick once more.

This time, rather than push her hands away, Aaron gripped her wrists and forced them against the small of her back. "Bad girl," he said, nipping at her shoulder as he spoke.

"Aaron. Stop messing around." She tried to break free but his hold tightened and he began to push her forward. He didn't stop until he had her facedown on the bed, his hand holding her immobile with her wrists still pressed against her back.

"I believe I was promised a *get off however you want* card."

His words sent a slight tremor through her as she realized in the heat of the lap dance moment, she'd handed him carte blanche. That was silly...and smart. Given his penchant for rough sex, she couldn't stop her body's response, couldn't wait to see where he would lead her now. The sound of a bag rustling roused her attention and she turned her head to confirm he'd retrieved the goodies from the sex shop with his free hand.

"Just remember the handcuffs were my choice... meaning I want to use them on you."

He chuckled and shook his head. "I'm cashing in on the promise you made at Swingers. One night of sex, my way. I think it's time you figured out exactly what kind of man you married."

"Aaron—"

"Hush. No more talking. Just obeying. And feeling. And coming."

She wanted to bitch about the *obeying* order, but the second two overshadowed the impulse.

Before she could say anything, he flipped her onto her back in the middle of the mattress. She only had a second to rub her wrists before he reclaimed them, pulling them over her head. Quickly and efficiently, he demonstrated his skills as a cop by handcuffing her to the bed. She wished the idea of being held captive didn't turn her on so much, but the truth was her nipples were hard enough to cut glass and she was dripping with her arousal. Aaron took in both those facts and grinned.

"Looks like I landed myself a bondage babe."

"You realize I'm not going to be able to let that name-calling go unpunished."

Aaron shrugged and grinned. "Threats won't work this time. All these years I've followed you to make sure you didn't get into trouble, always letting you call the shots. Tonight is my night, Riley, and I'm going to make every minute count."

She struggled against the handcuffs, but it was a token resistance at best. Every word he uttered drove her higher up the horny scale.

"So are you planning on talking me into an orgasm or do you actually have some plan to back up all this tough talk?"

He shook his head, undaunted by her taunt. "It won't work. There's no way you're going to top me from the bottom. Now close your mouth like a good little girl or I'm gonna gag you."

"You wouldn't dare."

He narrowed his eyes before looking around the room—she assumed—for something to use as a gag. "I'll be quiet," she conceded. It was hard enough not having use of her arms. She didn't want to lose her voice as well.

Aaron kissed her and as quickly as that, she forgot everything except how much she loved his kisses. The man certainly knew his way around a mouth. His tongue touched hers and she savored the minty tang of toothpaste on his breath. His hands engulfed her breasts, his lips taking a leisurely tour along her cheek, down her neck to her nipples. He sucked the hard tips into his mouth roughly, letting her feel the slight pressure of his teeth. She sucked in a harsh breath and squeezed her legs together, trying to create some sort of friction that would assuage her growing need.

He continued to play with her breasts until she was panting and begging for more. He was in no hurry and the siege he was laying on her body was clearly going to be a long one.

"God, Aaron," she cried as he took his time, licking and kissing a path along her stomach. "Suck my clit. Touch my pussy. *Do* something. You're killing me."

His breath as he chuckled tickled her mons, but he made no move to close in, instead he simply studied her body, getting a more than up close and personal look at her girlie bits.

She jumped when he touched her knee and he laughed. "On edge?"

She gave him a dirty look. "You can't leave me in these handcuffs forever, Aaron Young. You may want to remember that while you torment me. Turnabout is fair play in my book."

He pushed her legs apart and settled on his knees between them. Dragging one finger along her slit, he slowly touched her from ass to clit. Lifting his finger, he showed her the juice-covered digit. "Dessert." He sucked the finger into his mouth, cleaning it off. Jesus, every move he made was fucking hot. Like a sommelier sampling fine wine, he obviously approved of her flavor. Bending forward, he lightly kissed the tops of her thighs before he parted her folds with his fingers and went in for a good long taste.

She went into mindless mode as he alternated his movements, driving her insane with his talented mouth and fingers. While his teeth nipped and pressed at her clit, he fucked her with two thick fingers. When his tongue thrust into her channel, he used his fingers to torment her aching clit until she was gasping for breath. Three times he brought her to the brink of orgasm and three times he withheld the big ending, backing off despite her fluent cursing. She called him every foul name in the book, including cunt, when he moved away the fourth time.

"Tsk, tsk, tsk. Not very ladylike language, Mrs. Young."

"And when have I ever acted like a lady? Put your

mouth back down there and give me my orgasm, Aaron, or I'm gonna hurt you. Bad."

He chuckled and moved even farther away.

"Argh!" she cried in frustration.

Aaron ignored her growl and grabbed the bag of sex toys once more. There were only two more toys in the bag and she had more than a tiny hunch which one he'd go for. Her heart—already racing—sped up even more, beating triple time when he pulled out the vibrator and the butt plug.

"Be right back." She lay stunned for a moment, shocked he would leave her in such a state, but the sound of running water in the bathroom proved that while she was completely out of her mind with need, Aaron was in full possession of *his* faculties. He was washing the new toys, taking care of her safely. Just like always.

The realization brought tears to her eyes. God, she wasn't sure how she'd failed to see all of this over the years. Talk about taking someone for granted.

Never again, she decided. She'd never take him for granted again. She loved him. Loved him more than she'd ever loved another person and she was going to spend the rest of forever proving it to him.

Aaron returned to the room and she wondered what she'd given away with her face. He looked at her for a moment, really scrutinized her expression, and she knew she'd never be able to hide anything from him. He appeared to like what he saw because his face broke into a huge grin and he returned to the bed, leaning over to place a soft kiss on her lips.

"I love you too," he murmured.

She started to protest his cockiness, years of habit kicking in. Instead, she merely nodded.

"Now. Are you ready to play?"

She took a deep breath. "What the hell have we been doing for the last thirty minutes?"

"That was just foreplay. This is funplay."

He resumed his place between her knees and she gasped when he slid the vibrator into her pussy. No warning, no slow teasing, just functional motion. He wanted it inside her and he put it there.

"How does that feel? Are your arms okay?"

"I'm fine. All of me. More than fine."

He flashed the remote control at her and smiled wickedly. Pressing a button, he turned the toy on low gear. Not enough to push her over, but definitely enough to start her wiggling like a worm on a hook. "More."

He shook his head. "Not yet." He picked up her outstretched legs, lifting them at the knees and pushing them toward her chest. "Can you hold them there for a few minutes?"

She nodded. The position left her completely open to him. *Everything* was open to him. He grasped the lube and she bit her lip, trying to prepare herself for what came next. He studied her face and, for a moment, she thought he'd say something. Knowing Aaron, he probably wanted to get one more reassurance that she was okay with this. They looked at each other briefly and then he squeezed the lube onto his finger.

He winked at her as he wiggled the tip of his index finger at the entrance of her ass. "Ready?"

Apparently that was all the discussion they were going to have, as he slowly pushed the finger inside. It was tight and it pinched, but it certainly wasn't painful or uncomfortable. If anything the sensation was just sort of weird. She secretly grinned to herself. All these years she'd considered herself the worldly one in her relationship with Aaron. Who knew the gorgeous man would be introducing her to a whole new way to sin.

Thrusting in and out slowly, Aaron twice added more lube to her ass and then he slid in a second finger. This time the odd sensation turned to the slightest bit of pain, but again it wasn't unbearable. The speed on the vibrator kicked up a notch and suddenly the fingers in her ass didn't feel so bad at all. She was dripping wet and crying out for completion when he increased the vibrator's speed again, his fingers in her ass moving more quickly, deeper.

"God, Aaron," she gasped. "Please."

She closed her eyes to fight back tears when her pleading caused him to pull his fingers out of her completely. "No!"

The tip of something hard touched her anus and her eyes flew open. The plug. She'd forgotten about it. Aaron worked it inside her slowly and she sucked in a loud breath as the widest part breached her ass.

The second it was fully seated, Aaron cranked the vibrator up to its highest speed and she catapulted into the climax she'd withheld for nearly an hour.

For several moments, he simply watched as she

trembled in the aftermath. "So beautiful," he whispered when he turned off the vibrator and slid it out, only to replace it with his own gorgeous, thick cock.

He made love to her leisurely, the impact of being doubly filled driving her higher than she would have believed. She came once more as he moved inside, kissing her, touching her, murmuring the most incredible words she'd ever heard.

"Come with me," she invited, and he closed his eyes as if savoring the sound of her voice. He pressed in just two more times, the thrusts firm and deep, then he gave himself up to the inevitable. Reaching between them, he rubbed her clit, dragging her along for the ride as well.

The last thing she heard as she drifted off to sleep was Aaron's light snoring. She smiled. It was the first time he'd ever fallen asleep before her. She liked the sound. She liked it a lot.

IT WAS WELL after noon when they woke up the following day. Given the fact they hadn't gone to sleep until nearly dawn, Aaron wasn't surprised they'd slept so late. They remained in bed for several drowsy minutes, neither of them energetic enough to move. They'd had a long day yesterday and unless they found Trev and Bella right away, today would prove to be just as long.

"So what's the plan?" Riley asked.

"Same as yesterday, I guess. We'll cruise through

the casinos again, hit Swingers to see if Bella called. Maybe check in with Bubbles and that clerk at Sal's again."

"Shit."

"Yeah," he agreed.

"I'm hungry." Riley rubbed her stomach and Aaron shook his head.

"What else is new?"

"Very funny. We didn't eat much yesterday, you know. One late lunch and a couple hash browns. That was it."

"I know."

She slowly stood up and pulled on her jeans. He watched her progress, admiring her sleek, trim figure. She had curves in all the right places. He didn't decide to follow suit and get dressed too until she was completely covered.

Show over.

He smiled to himself. Riley burned hotter than a bonfire in bed. He bet he could make her forget about her hunger in less than a minute.

His stomach growled. Loudly. Shit. He was hungry too.

"Let's hit the all-you-can-eat buffet next door," she suggested.

"What is it with you and all-you-can-eat places?"

She looked at him as if he were stupid. "Um, hello? All. You. Can. Eat. It's the concept I like."

"How much do you think you can eat? Your stomach's not much bigger than your fist."

"I'm *really* hungry," she stressed.

"You always say that. Then you eat one plate of food. Seems like a waste of money to me."

"Waste or not, that's where we're going."

He shrugged. "Fine. Regardless of your eating habits, I'm pretty sure I could put a serious dent in their bar. I really *am* starving."

"Worked up an appetite, did you?"

"Hell yeah and I have every intention of working this meal off later. With you. In that bed. Lead the way."

They opened the door just as Johanna was about to knock. Aaron fought back a groan. He'd been hoping they could avoid the woman until they found Trev. So much for that fantasy.

"Where the fuck is he?" Johanna bellowed. "You said you would send him up to my room. I fucking took a bath, ate room service twice and watched ten hours of *Sex in the City*. TBS was having a marathon. Did you hear that? TBS. Not HBO. Fucking shows were cut to ribbons and I still watched. I finally fell asleep around midnight only to wake up alone."

"Sorry, Jo. We should have called you, but we were sort of tied up." Riley sent Aaron a wicked grin and he had to bite his lip not to laugh at her reminder of exactly how he'd tied her up last night.

"Yeah, well. I got up, went down for breakfast and just spent the last three hours playing the slots. My eyeballs feel wiggly from watching those symbols roll by for so long. Enough is enough. Why don't you tell me what you obviously didn't tell me yesterday? Where the fuck is Trevor?"

Riley sighed and Aaron knew the next few minutes were bound to be uncomfortable. And potentially dangerous. He suddenly wished he had brought his weapon with him. He glanced to the left and saw Jo's baseball bat tucked securely in the corner. A quick calculation proved he could get to it before she did, so he relaxed a bit.

"I'm afraid you aren't going to like this." And Riley told her the whole sordid story. "So we've been trying to find him, but we just haven't had any luck. I'm sure if he knew about the baby, he'd be back in a New York minute, begging your forgiveness and trying to make amends. You know Trev, Jo. He's not a bad guy really. Just a little impulsive."

Johanna didn't reply and for a minute, Aaron was worried she was going into shock.

"Are you okay, Jo? You know, Riley and I were just about to hit the buffet next door. Why don't you come with us? You're eating for two now and it wouldn't do you or the baby any good to get worked up about this. I'm sure it will all still work out okay."

"No, thank you. I'm not hungry." Jo's voice was calm and strong and he studied her face closely. Hell, all in all, Aaron thought she'd taken the news fairly well. She politely thanked Riley for being honest with her, calmly informed them she was going to find her husband and murder the faithless motherfucker, and then she said goodbye.

Riley and Aaron watched her retreat down the hall from the doorway of their room. Johanna smashed the vase sitting on the table by the elevator. Minimal damage really, considering it was a jilted Johanna Blankenship they were watching.

"You thinking what I'm thinking?" Riley asked when the elevator doors closed.

"Yep," he replied. "We'd better find Trev before she does or there won't be any pieces of the poor man left to bury."

"Yeah, well, even knowing that, I'm still hitting the all-you-can-eat."

Aaron nodded. "Agreed. Let's go."

They were almost to the front entrance to the hotel when Johnny stumbled in the sliding doors. He looked as if he'd seen better nights. His thick dark hair was sticking up at odd angles and the bow tie on his black tuxedo lay loose around his neck.

When he spotted them, he raised his hand and called out Riley's name. Aaron saw more than a few people in the lobby do a double take, trying to decide if they were really seeing an extremely hungover Wayne Newton.

"She quit her fucking job," he said.

Riley nodded. "I know. We went by Swingers last night."

There were angry tears in Johnny's eyes as he spoke. "She wouldn't quit to marry me and have kids, but she'll drop that gig fast enough for some rich guy."

"Trev's not exactly rich," Riley said, but Aaron placed a hand on her shoulder and shook his head.

"All this time I thought she was addicted to the spotlight, to being a star. I understood that because she still came home to me every night. It wasn't the job," he said, his voice laced with agony. "It was me. I wasn't good enough for her."

"Oh Johnny." Riley reached out and took his hand in hers. "I'm so sorry. Really I am. We were just going to head next door to the all-you-can-eat buffet. Why don't you come with us? My treat."

Johnny accepted her comfort for only a moment before he shook off her hand and raised a pointed finger at them. "I'm gonna find that asshole friend of yours and I'm gonna kill him. Kill him for stealing my Bella away from me!"

Before they could try to talk him down, he turned and stormed away.

"Wow." Riley turned to look at him. "This sucks."

He nodded. "Yep. Trev's in a whole world of hurt."

"We still hitting the buffet?"

He grasped her hand and headed for the street again. "Hell yeah."

CHAPTER NINE

As they walked out of the casino, Riley's cell phone rang.

"Hello?" she answered.

"Riley?"

"Yep. Bubbles?"

"Hey."

Riley frowned at the woman's dejected tone. When she'd left Bubbles last night, the woman had been floating on air and confidence. Her voice now betrayed serious depression. "Oh shit. What's wrong? Didn't you get the job?"

"Oh yeah. I got it."

"Woohoo!" Riley pulled the phone away from her ear and looked at Aaron. "Bubbles got the stripper job."

Putting the phone back to her ear, she started to congratulate her new friend. "That's awesome. I'm—"

"I got it and lost it." Bubbles halted her rejoicing mid-sentence.

"Lost it?" She pulled the phone away again and shook her head. "She lost it."

"How?" he asked.

"How?" she asked into the phone.

"That cunt Bella fucked me over."

"Bella?" Riley asked.

Aaron frowned. "Bella? Is she back?"

"Apparently the cunt showed up at the club and begged for her job back this morning. That loser Louis gave it to her. He just called to tell me the lap-dance job was no longer necessary since he had his star back. I *rocked* that place last night. If you don't count the broken chair. And the three spilled drinks. And there was the issue with my elbow and that guy's eye, but other than that, I rocked it."

"Is she still at the club?"

"How the hell should I know?" Bubbles yelled. "I'm not there yet."

"Yet?"

"I'm looking for that whore and when I find her, I'm gonna kick her scrawny ass from here to Kansas."

"Listen, Bubbles. Why don't you take a little while? Calm down. Aaron and I are going to the all-you-can-eat place next door to our hotel. Why don't you come have a late lunch with us?"

"I can't eat at a time like this. I'm too upset. I'll get gas."

"Well, I really think you should forget about the stripper job. If they don't want you, then you need to just say fuck it. That manager clearly doesn't know a good thing when he sees it. I'd be surprised if he didn't run the club into the ground before the year's out."

"Yeah, you're right. Louis is a fucking loser and an idiot to boot."

"Exactly. Feel better?"

"No. I'm gonna go get my hair done. I need a new color. A new color always cheers me up."

"Sounds like a good idea. Purple would look nice with your skin tone. Call me later if you want."

"I will. Thanks, Riley."

"Bye, Bubbles."

"What was that about?" Aaron asked.

"Bella showed up at the club this morning asking for her job back. Louis gave it to her. And gave Bubbles the boot. Apparently there were a few small mishaps."

Aaron rolled his eyes. "Of course there were. Let me guess, she's looking to kill Trev too?"

"Nope, she's after Bella's blood."

Aaron seemed impressed. "Well, there's a nice twist on a classic. I thought today was Trev's day to die."

Riley shrugged. "Apparently he's not going down alone." They stood outside the restaurant and paused for a minute. "We're still going in, right?"

"There's nothing we can do about the Trev and Bella situation right now. We still don't know where they are. We can head back to the strip club tonight and maybe we'll catch Trev there while Bella's dancing. Warn him Jo's in town and on the warpath. You realize the only reason Bella would want her job back is because Trevor lost all his winnings?"

"Jeez. You're right. What a tool."

Aaron nodded. "So, here's the plan. After we do our good deed of warning Trev he's in imminent danger, we're locking ourselves in that hotel room, taking the phone off the hook and having wild monkey sex until the coming of the next Ice Age. And I don't mean the movie."

Riley laughed. "Awesome plan. Come on. Let's go eat."

As they entered the restaurant, the hostess led them to their table, took their drink orders and told them to help themselves to the bar.

"We'll go monochromatic."

"Jesus," Aaron muttered. "Do you have to do this every time we hit one of these places?"

"It's fun. I dibs anything that's a shade of yellow. The Starch Special. Macaroni and cheese, mashed potatoes, creamed corn and a roll."

"Riley. I'm not playing."

"Why not?"

"Because you always try to stick me with green. I'm not walking down this food bar and passing up all the good stuff just so everything on my plate will match. I'm really hungry."

Riley studied the food. "You could probably manage red. There's spaghetti, barbeque ribs and pepperoni pizza."

Aaron considered her suggestion. "That doesn't sound bad, actually."

She grinned and kissed him on the cheek.

"What was that for?"

"You always play along with me."

He grimaced. "Your pop calls it 'indulging you' and he doesn't seem to think it's a good thing."

"Well, in this one instance, my pop is wrong."

They walked along the bar, getting their monochromatic meals and laughing at the strange looks they were receiving from the other diners as they debated whether certain foods were indeed red or yellow.

As they headed back to their table, they were just about to sit down when she spotted Trev and a woman she assumed was Bella sitting at a table in the corner.

"Damn. You weren't kidding about her tits."

Aaron looked up, confused, and followed her gaze. "Shit. Guess it's true what they say. You always find something the minute you stop looking. You know, they don't look happy."

Riley snorted. "They look fucking sunburned. Jeez. Trev's red as a beet."

"Wonder what they're arguing about?"

Riley grinned. "Probably pissed off because they didn't pack sunscreen."

Aaron sighed and set his tray of food on the table. "I guess we should go let Trev know about Jo."

Riley looked down at her tray and shook her head. "Nope. You know what? Fuck him. I've wasted the first two days of my honeymoon on that dumbass and I'm hungry. My food is warm now. If we go over there, you know as well as I do it'll turn into some big ugly scene and my lovely macaroni and cheese will go stiff."

Aaron crossed his arms over his chest. "Riley. Jo,

Bubbles and Johnny are on the warpath. We need to warn—"

"Hey, you two! Changed my mind about the new hairdo. Eating my way into oblivion is just as good as purple hair for a pick-me-up. Let me get a plate and I'll be right back." They turned to watch as Bubbles sauntered up to the bar and starting piling up her plate.

"Shit," Riley muttered. "Thank God she was looking our way. She missed seeing Bella altogether."

"You think that will hold true when she comes back?" Aaron asked. "We've gotta get Bella and Trev out of here or we're gonna have Armageddon on our hands. You remember what that clerk at Sal's said. Those two women get in the same room together and shit gets broken. There are kids in here."

"Okay. Listen, I'll—"

"I decided you two were right."

Riley looked up to see Johanna standing next to her.

"I'm eating for two and I can't let Trev's wandering dick endanger the life of my baby. Jerry Springer has made that point a million times on his show. I'll go grab a plate." She glanced down at their plates and laughed. "Doing the one-color deal, eh?"

Riley nodded numbly.

"Well, I'm not eating one color. I'm eating every color…twice. I have to think of the baby."

Riley looked at Aaron and gave him a crooked grin as Jo walked away. "Jesus. All we need is for Johnny to walk in and we'll have a trifecta."

Aaron didn't laugh at her joke. Instead, he pointed

toward the front door of the restaurant. Sure enough, Johnny was walking their way.

"Can't find your friend. He's a slippery fucker," he said, rubbing his temple. "Feeling a little sick. Must be the heat."

"Or the booze," Aaron muttered.

"Yeah, well. I think food will help. Still your treat, right?"

Johnny headed to the food bar without waiting for their answer.

Riley watched the three unsuspecting people jostling for food position at the bar and then glanced back at Bella and Trevor, so wrapped up in their argument they didn't see World War III descending on them.

She giggled. She couldn't help it. "Wow. This is gonna be so funny."

"Dammit, Riley. Do *not* start laughing. We've got five mentally unstable people here."

"Think we should evacuate the building?" She laughed harder at her joke, but Aaron continued to scowl.

"You distract them while I go over and tell Trev and Bella to get the hell out of here."

Riley nodded her agreement, unable to speak as her laughter bubbled over to the boiling point. Jesus. She really couldn't stop laughing and tears began to stream over her cheeks. Whether it was exhaustion, frustration or the fact that her entire being had been on overload since her drunken elopement to Aaron, she felt all the stress and craziness of the past two days escaping in uncontrollable laughter.

"What's so funny?" Bubbles asked.

Riley couldn't speak to answer. Instead she snorted and laughed harder. Putting up one finger, she fought hard to catch her breath. Aaron was shaking his head, but she could see he was fighting back his own laughter. They were screwed. They both knew it.

"S-s-sorry," she gasped, taking a deep breath. "Got the giggles there."

Aaron nodded, his face breaking into a wide grin. "I can see that. Let the cards fall where they may?"

Riley shrugged and agreed. "Our offensive line sucks. Time to switch to defensive maneuvers."

Bubbles was staring at them oddly. "What?"

"Nothing," Aaron said as the occasional odd giggle continued to escape Riley's lips. "Let's just eat."

"What the fuck is *she* doing here?" Bubbles' tone and angry question alerted Riley that she'd finally spotted her nemesis.

"That didn't take long," Riley muttered. The fury in her new friend's eyes quickly dispelled the humor she'd been feeling. Shit. She wasn't sure their defense was going to be strong enough.

"Bubbles," Riley said, standing up and stepping in front of the woman when she started toward Bella's table. "Listen. I need you to sit and calm down. Going over there right now isn't going to solve anything."

"Of course it will," Bubbles screeched. "Me rearranging that cunt's face will solve everything."

Bubbles sidestepped Riley and stalked across the room.

"Uh-oh." Aaron was looking at the food bar. Johanna and Johnny had also caught sight of their prey and were crossing the room, food trays in hand, to confront them.

Riley threw up her hands. "Let's go."

She and Aaron rushed over to Bella and Trev's table. The couple was no longer arguing and instead looked shell-shocked as they were surrounded by the enemy on three sides.

"Jo?" Trev asked stupidly.

Bella burst into tears when she saw her ex. "Johnny!"

For a brief moment, Riley foolishly thought they may be all right. They'd all sit down like rational, civilized people and things would work out. Bubbles dashed that hope with one swing of her tray. She dumped all her food onto an unsuspecting Bella's lap. Bella hissed like a wet cat, picking up her glass of iced tea and tossing the liquid in Bubbles' face.

Unfortunately, Riley had chosen to stand a little too closely to Bubbles and half the liquid covered her as well.

"Dammit, Bella," Riley said. "I was supposed to be in Vegas for two days. I didn't pack enough clothes for you to start tossing shit on—"

Her words died when a snowball of mashed potatoes struck her mid-chest.

"Oops," Trev said. "I was aiming for that crazy woman." He pointed at Bubbles, who was now chucking rolls and food from their table and surrounding ones like a soldier lobs grenades. Trev raised his hand in an attempt to dodge the bread and French fries raining down on him. "Make her stop throwing shit, Riley!"

Riley turned to block Bubbles' view of the table, reaching to grab the woman's hands. "Bubbles, stop it! The manager is gonna call the cops. Do you want to go to jail?"

"I want that bitch to stand up and fight me, fair and square."

"Who you callin' a bitch?" Bella shouted from the table. Before Riley could turn, she felt something very cold and slimy hit her back and begin sliding down her T-shirt.

"What the hell?" She turned around to find Bella dipping her spoon into a bowl of ice cream, preparing to launch more of her hot fudge sundae.

"Put it down," Riley said. Bella paused for a moment. "Put. It. *Down*."

Riley started to yell at Aaron for not stepping in to help her but one glance to her left proved he was fighting his own losing battle. He had his arms wrapped around Johanna from behind as the woman flailed about, attempting to batter Trev with her purse, her fists, her feet. Trev was pleading with her to calm down, his hands constantly moving, alternating between covering his face and his privates. She was putting up one helluva fight.

The sound of sirens outside had the effect of someone dousing them with a hose, and the fight went out of them. Jo hung limply in Aaron's arms. Bella put her hands in her lap and Bubbles sank into a chair at another table.

Two policemen came in and the manager pointed at them.

"Great," Riley heard one of the cops mutter as they walked up. "Bubbles and Bella. Again. What did we do to deserve this?"

AN HOUR LATER, the seven of them found themselves back on the street—sticky, hot and three hundred and thirty-seven dollars and fifty-four cents poorer. Somehow that was the price tag the manager put on the destruction they'd wrought in the restaurant. Luckily, Aaron had managed to talk the Vegas cops out of citing them all for disorderly conduct.

"What now?" Riley asked. She wanted to go back to the hotel and clean up. Unfortunately she was surrounded by too many crazy people looking to her for answers. There was no way she was going to risk taking them someplace where they could destroy anything else. She was officially broke.

Aaron pointed to a small café that had outdoor seating. "Do you all think you could sit at that café without throwing fists, food or drinks at each other?"

They all nodded wearily and proceeded down the street in a pack. Riley ignored the looks of passersby. She knew they all probably looked as if they'd escaped from some asylum. They were covered in food. Riley's hair was stuck together in three places with dried mashed potatoes. Bella's long blonde hair was coated with tomato sauce and Bubbles' hot pink 'do was flatter than Riley'd ever seen it, weighted down by ice cream and hot fudge.

The guys had actually fared worse. In addition to the food stains, Trev had a fat lip. Aaron was going to have a black eye by morning, thanks to an accidental headbutt from Jo, who looked like a reject in a white T-shirt contest from the pitcher of soda Trev had lobbed at her in an attempt to calm her down.

Surprisingly the hostess at the café agreed to seat them. She gave them one of the patio tables and brought them all glasses of water.

"Okay," Aaron said, when they were all seated at last. "Here's what happens now. Trev, you and Bella are gonna tell us where you were for the last two days. The rest of us," he gave an especially stern look at Jo, who looked contrite, "will listen. We're not speaking until their story is finished. Then we'll all calmly say our piece and go our separate ways. Got it?" Everyone nodded and Riley grinned.

For a moment she saw her future, saw Aaron solving fights between their children this way.

Children. She'd never considered having kids, but watching Aaron handle five unruly adults drove home to her how much she *did* want them. Lots of them. Maybe she'd try to break her parents' record and go for eight. The thought made her smile and she saw Aaron give her a quizzical, confused look.

"I'll tell you later," she mouthed.

"So," Aaron prompted, and Trev began his tale of woe while the rest of them listened in dumbfounded silence.

After leaving Riley and Aaron at the blackjack table, they'd gone up to his hotel room. Unfortunately, guilt over cheating on his wife had left Trev unable to perform, so they'd decided to hit the gambling tables again instead. Bella had been blowing off steam, angry with Johnny for trying to pressure her into marriage.

Riley figured Bella and Trev had found a sympathetic ear in each other. They'd only been at the slot machines for a few minutes when Trev hit the jackpot, winning a hundred grand.

"To celebrate, I took Bella out and bought her a fur coat."

Jo narrowed her eyes but Trev raised his hand quickly. "I was gonna get you one too, honey, but since I didn't want to carry it around with me all night, I was gonna go back later."

His answer seemed to appease his wife, but Riley knew better. In addition to the fur coat, he and Bella had stopped by Sal's Sex Shop and, if the note he'd left her at the front desk was to be believed, he'd intended to marry Bella. Obviously, too much time spent in each other's presence had proven them incompatible and Trev had had a change of heart. He was putting out some serious ass-kissing vibes and Riley tried not to be disgusted by the fact Jo was falling for it. Sheesh. Stupid woman.

"Anyway, Bella knew of some guys who hosted a nightly poker game with a big pot, one where you needed five thousand bucks just to enter. She said we should go, make a fortune so we could quit working and live the rest of our lives like fat cats."

"You took him to Vinnie's place?" Johnny asked.

Bella nodded guiltily.

"Vinnie the Snake?" Bubbles added, her eyes wide as she crossed herself reverently. "Jesus, *chica*."

Riley looked at Bella. "So let me get this straight. You called and quit your job *before* this Vinnie the Snake's poker game? Didn't that seem a bit premature to you?"

Bella shrugged. "I thought we were on a roll. We were feeling real lucky."

"You lost all the money the very first night, didn't you?" Aaron asked.

Trev nodded. "In less than two hours, I was twelve thousand in the hole. Apparently those guys didn't believe in IOUs and I didn't have that kind of cash on me. I told them I was good for it, but they got sort of pissed."

Johnny shook his head. "Vinnie the Snake don't get pissed. He gets even."

Bella took up the tale at this point. "They took my fur coat and then they threw us in the back of this black sedan and drove us out of town. I thought they were going to kill us." She looked at Johnny, tears streaming down her face. "I thought I'd never see you again."

Johnny reached over and took her hand. "It's okay, muffin. You're here. Johnny will take care of everything."

Riley rolled her eyes. She hated when people referred to themselves in third person. Aaron winked at her. He knew all about that particular pet peeve of hers. He leaned forward and whispered in her ear, "Aaron thinks you look hot with mashed potatoes in your hair."

She narrowed her eyes. "Riley's gonna kick you in the balls if you don't behave yourself."

He chuckled.

"So what happened next?" Bubbles asked. Riley could see her new friend was enthralled with their adventure and hanging on the edge of her seat. "Did they beat you with rubber hoses? Bury you alive in shallow graves? Strip you naked and cover your bodies in fire ants?"

Riley gestured to them. "Jesus, Bubbles. You need to stop watching mafia movies. Look at them. Do they look like they've been stripped and beaten?"

Trev shook his head. "No. They didn't do any of that. They dumped us off in the middle of the damn desert. Left us there. We spent most of yesterday walking back. Had to sleep outside last night. Kept feeling like shit was crawling on me and I'm chafed on account of there's so much sand in my ass. First thing this morning we caught a break. A guy in a pickup truck stopped and let us ride in his truck bed. He brought us the rest of the way into the city."

"He was taking garbage to the dump," Bella said distastefully and Trev sighed angrily.

"It was a *ride*, Bella. Maybe you'd rather still be walking?"

"All I'm saying is, I'm a lady. He could have offered me a seat inside the cab and moved that stupid big dog of his to the back with you."

"You're lucky he even stopped, you silly—"

Aaron whistled. "Story finished?"

They nodded.

Riley suddenly thought of something. "Hey, how the hell did you plan to pay for that all-you-can-eat lunch if Vinnie and his thugs took all your money?"

"They didn't take it all," Bella said, reaching down her top. "I always keep an emergency fifty tucked in my bra."

Aaron narrowed his eyes and took the damp bill out of her hand.

"Hey!" she protested.

"That still doesn't cover your share of the destruction back at the restaurant." Riley figured that was as much of the money they'd ever get back. The rest was riding on Aaron's credit card until the end of the month.

Bella looked at Bubbles. "I called Louis as soon as we hit town and asked for my job back. He said you filled in for me. Thanks."

Bubbles seemed taken aback by Bella's sincere gratitude. She shrugged and appeared embarrassed. "Sure. No problem."

"Johnny," Bella said. "When I was in that car and I thought I was gonna get killed, I realized I've been wrong to say no to you. If you'll still have me, I'd like to marry you."

Johnny's eyes lit up. "And kids?"

Bella bit her lip. "Can we maybe just do the wedding thing first? Figure out the kids later?"

Riley rolled her eyes. *Oh yeah. That's a good plan.* Who gets married without talking about all the important stuff? She looked at Aaron and thought about her desire for lots of kids. *Shit.*

Johnny kissed Bella and the two of them stood up. "We sure can, muffin. Why don't we go home and celebrate?"

They said their goodbyes while Riley looked around the table. "And then there were five," she muttered.

"Jo," Trev started. "I've been a dumbass."

Johanna nodded. "You can say that again. But you're *my* dumbass."

Trevor's eyes lit up. "Does that mean you'll take me back?"

"Gonna have to. Somebody's gotta be this baby's daddy." She rubbed her stomach and Riley thought Trev actually went pale beneath his sunburn.

"Baby?"

"I'm pregnant."

Trev raised his fist in the air and let out a holler loud enough that it must've had people from three blocks away turning their heads. They all laughed as he stood up, picked up his wife and spun her around. "Come on. I'm taking my gal out for a fancy supper. I'm gonna be a daddy!"

They said goodbye and walked off hand in hand.

Bubbles sighed sadly.

"You okay, Bubbles?" Riley asked.

"Two more happy endings. And here I am still

stuck in this shithole city, hooking for a living. You know, I'm starting to think my Richard Gere's not coming to save me."

"So maybe you should go out and look for him." Riley leaned closer. "Come back to Baltimore with us. Start over fresh in a new city."

"Doing what?"

"You can work at my family's pub. I need an assistant in the kitchen and my sister Keira's knocked up again. We'll need another waitress."

"I don't have a lot of money saved up. Costs a lot of money to keep me looking so stylish. I wouldn't be able to afford a place to stay for a while, even with the offer of a job."

Riley laughed. "I know a place that's about to be empty that you can rent for super cheap until you get your feet under you."

"Um, Riley," Aaron interrupted. "This place?"

"I'm not living in your apartment, Aaron."

He frowned. "Why not?"

"Do you want a list? Number one, it's tiny. Number two, there's no air conditioning. It's the beginning of June. Do you know how hot Baltimore gets in July and August? I'm not sweating my ass off. On top of that, you don't have a tub—just a shower, there's like zero parking around your neighborhood and the commute to the pub would be murder."

Aaron grinned. "Is that all?"

She gave him an exasperated look, but he just waved her off with a chuckle. "So where are we living?"

"Until we find a place of our own, I thought we'd stay with Pop, in Tristan's old room." She didn't want to admit the idea of leaving the old guy alone without proper warning was worrying her. She knew she and Aaron would move out eventually and Pop would be on his own, but she wanted to give him time to get used to that idea.

Aaron looked at her for a long time and she wondered how far he—or she, for that matter—would take this argument.

"Fine. We'll stay with your pop. That's closer to the police station anyway and it's not like I own anything of value. I furnished my whole apartment with stuff picked up at garage sales and the Salvation Army Surplus Store."

She smiled, overwhelmed with relief. "Really? You sure you don't mind."

He leaned close and kissed her on the end of her nose. "I don't mind. I'm crazy about your pop, you know that. We'll stay with him for a while, save up some money, and take our time finding a house. One with a yard."

"A house sounds awesome."

"So the issue of where we're living is taken care of, but are you seriously planning to take a hooker home to wait tables at your family's pub? Sorry, Bubbles, no offense intended."

"None taken," Bubbles replied.

"Yeah. That's what I'm planning," Riley answered.

Aaron looked exasperated and Riley laughed. She

loved having this effect on him. "Don't you think you should run this idea by your pop?"

"Fine. I'll call him. But I'm telling you right now, he won't mind." Riley was certain she could convince Pop to let Bubbles work at the pub. "So it's settled," Riley said.

"Awesome!" Bubbles rose quickly and headed for the sidewalk. "I'm gonna start packing up. Maybe get that fresh hair dye after all. A new start definitely calls for a new color."

"Definitely," Riley agreed, saying goodbye.

"I'll call you later, Riley," Bubbles said before walking away.

"Your pop's gonna kill you. You know that, right? And your brothers are gonna want to hurt me for letting you bring a hooker home."

Riley shrugged. "She's a nice person who's down on her luck. My family is awesome. They'll wanna help her. I just know it."

Aaron wanted to contradict her, but he couldn't. Her words were the truth. The Collins family was nothing if not compassionate and kind.

"So," Riley said, leaning back against her chair. "What's next?"

Aaron grinned at her. "Honeymoon boom-boom."

CHAPTER TEN

They entered their hotel room hand in hand, walking slowly. Now that tragedy had been averted, both of them were feeling the benefit of time finally being on their side.

As Aaron closed the door behind them and started across the room, Riley remained by the entrance. "Hey. Aren't you forgetting something?"

He turned to look at her, confusion in his eyes. "I don't think so."

She gestured at the door behind her. "Has the passion already died, sugar? Where's my hot sex against the door?"

He grinned, coming back to stand in front of her. "I thought you might prefer a shower first. We *are* sort of sticky."

"True that." She reached up and lightly ran her finger along the bruise darkening beneath his eye. "Does this hurt?"

He shook his head. "No, it's—"

"I love you." She blurted the words, unable to hold them in any longer. "I really, really love you."

He leaned closer to her, his face covered with the most genuine smile she'd ever seen. "I know that, Riley."

"It's just…I've never said those words to you and I wanted to." Her comment sounded inane and she fought against the urge to roll her eyes at herself.

"I'm glad you wanted to say it. In fact, if you wanted to say it, oh…maybe fifty, sixty times a day for the next century or so, I wouldn't complain."

She huffed out a breathy laugh. "Not too greedy, are you, sugar?"

"With you, I'm the greediest man on earth. I want everything. Your heart, your body, your friendship, your soft cries as you come and as many babies as you're willing to give me."

"Eight."

He looked at her quizzically. "Eight?"

"Thought maybe we could try to beat my folks' record."

Aaron tweaked her nipple through her T-shirt before engulfing the entire breast in his large palm. "It wouldn't be a hardship to try."

"Horny bastard." Her teasing words ended with a slight squeak when Aaron cupped her mound with his other hand and rubbed hard.

He pushed her back against the door in a move she was beginning to crave more than Saturday nights. Leaning forward, he kissed her thoroughly and she wrapped her arms around his waist, pulling him even closer. Sometimes she thought she could pull him completely inside her and it still wouldn't be close enough.

For several moments, they kissed and touched. When Aaron pulled away, their shirts stuck together and they laughed.

"Shower," she said. "We definitely need a shower. And I hate to break this to you, but I'm out of clean clothes. We may have to run out later for a little shopping. And for food. We didn't get to eat again."

Aaron nodded. "We'll order room service. Less opportunity for mishaps."

Taking her hand, he led her to the bathroom, where they took the longest hot shower in the history of indoor plumbing. It took three shampoos to get all the mashed potatoes out of her hair, but Riley didn't mind since it was Aaron doing the scrubbing. His hands, lightly massaging her scalp, felt like heaven.

Walking back to the bedroom, they crawled beneath the sheets and cuddled. It seemed neither of them was in a hurry to rush the evening and for the first time since they'd eloped, Riley felt like she was on a real honeymoon. Lying in his arms and making plans for the future, Riley knew she'd been blessed in this marriage she didn't even know she wanted. Hell, she still couldn't even remember the wedding part. As soon as they got home, she was going to have to sit down and watch the DVD he'd bought.

"You know, this might sound silly, but there's a part

of me that sort of thinks my mom set this marriage up."

"Your mom?" Aaron asked.

Sunday Collins had passed away from cancer when Riley was only ten years old, but her memories of her mother were solid in her mind. She recalled helping her in the restaurant kitchen, listening and watching as her mother shared all her secret recipes and tricks of the trade with her. Riley knew from a very young age that she wanted to be just like her mother when she grew up, knew she wanted to create masterpieces with food.

"She told me once she could see inside your heart."

Aaron looked down at her. "You never told me that."

Riley shrugged. She tried to discreetly brush away a tear, but Aaron grasped her wrist, pulled her hand away. "Let it fall."

She looked at him, confused.

"You always stop the tears; always find a way to twist everything into a joke. Don't do that this time."

She blinked rapidly. He was right. Humor had always been her life preserver. Well, humor and Aaron.

She decided it was time to tell him the one thing she'd never told anyone.

"A few days before she died, my mom called me into her room. She was in a lot of pain at the time, but she didn't want to take the drugs because they left her too out of it. She knew her time was limited and she was trying very hard to say all the things she wanted to say. I think she was trying to help me—help all of us—put our lives in some sort of order. There she was—seven kids between the ages of nine and eighteen—and she was dying."

"That sounds like your mom. She was an amazing woman."

Riley smiled. "She was the best."

"You're a lot like her."

Riley shook her head at his words but he disregarded her dismissal.

"You are. You have her talent for cooking. You make magic in the kitchen. I think you both use food to show your love for your family and friends. You have her strength of will and you have her love for life. She'd be proud of the woman you've become, Riley."

Every word he spoke felt like a gift and Riley held on to each of them tightly. "I hope so. The day she called me in, she said, 'Hold on to Aaron. He's your true friend and he loves you. I know he'll keep you safe for me.'"

Aaron reared back, shock evident in his features. "How could she have known that? We were ten."

Riley shook her head. "I don't know. I just know she was right. You've never left my side, never failed to be there for me when I needed you. I love you so much."

He kissed her as she gave in to the tears and, for several long moments, held her tightly, kissing, wiping the tears away until there weren't any more.

"Aaron," she whispered. "Will you make love to me?"

He tightened his grip around her shoulders briefly before turning and rising over her. She opened her legs and welcomed him in. As he slowly thrust inside her, she felt the rightness of it.

They came together, not in a flurry of passion and heat but with the same comforting, peaceful style they'd shared through years of friendship. Aaron kissed her as he gently rocked inside her. Their eyes met and held, neither of them willing to drop the connection. She wrapped her arms around his neck and her legs around his waist. She wanted to hold on to him with everything she had, everything that she was.

"You're so soft," Aaron whispered as he stroked the skin at her waist.

She smiled, moving her hands to his shoulders, squeezing the firm muscles she found there. "And you're so hard."

He rubbed his nose against hers and pushed into her deeper. "Are you complaining?"

"Hell no. Hard is good." She thrust her hips upward to meet his next return and both of them gasped at the pleasure the movement produced. "Hard is *really* good."

He kissed her for several moments. When he pulled away, she reached up to cup his cheek, his beloved face hovering just above hers. "I was the world's biggest fool not to see what was standing right in front of me all this time. You've always been with me, watching over me, taking care of me. I honestly don't know what I've done to deserve you, Aaron. Hell, I'm not sure I *do* deserve you, but I swear I have no intention of ever taking you for granted again."

Aaron kissed her forehead and moved inside once

more, before holding still within her. "You act like this is a one-sided deal. Riley, I can't imagine my life without you. You make me a better person."

She giggled, but he thrust inside once more, quickly turning her chuckle to a moan.

"I'm being serious," he said.

She leaned up and nipped his chin lightly. "Sugar, no one's ever accused me of making them a better person. In high school, I was voted 'Person Most Likely to Share a Jail Cell', remember?"

He laughed, the action rocking him even deeper and she gasped. She'd never had a full-blown conversation in the midst of sex, but with Aaron, it seemed so natural…and hot.

He ran his hand through her hair. "I remember," he said. "But I'm standing by what I said, you've made my life better. Look at me, Riley. I'm not exactly the world's most spontaneous person."

She raised her eyebrows, her grin showing she agreed with his assessment.

"If not for you, I'd never have bought my motorcycle."

She tightened her legs around his waist and pushed her hips toward him. "Mmm, have I told you lately how hot I think that bike is?"

He met her push with a quick, hard thrust of his own. "You've told me. Daily. You're still not driving it."

She stuck out her tongue. He bent forward and sucked it into his mouth, kissing her once more. She'd never been a huge fan of kissing, but Aaron was damn good at it.

He pulled back after several moments and she could see he wasn't finished. "You were the one who convinced me to get my tattoo."

Her hand instinctively went to his right shoulder blade, fingering the tiny Celtic knot she knew was there. Interwoven with the knot was the name of Aaron's twin sister, Alise, who died in childbirth.

She stroked it gently and he moved into her once more. She'd asked him to make love to her, but this felt like so much more. While his body took hers, his words claimed her heart, her mind, her soul. He was inside every part of her, deeper than anyone had ever been and she felt like the most cherished person on earth.

"I'm not even sure I would have gone into the Police Academy if not for you. You make me laugh every day, Riley. I could have the shittiest day in history and you would still find a way to make everything okay. So enough of this *I don't deserve you* garbage."

Obviously he was finished trying to convince her with words. Before she could respond, he started moving, slowly at first, but soon his thrusts grew harder, faster, deeper. She dug her fingers into his shoulders, simply to find something to anchor her to this place, this time, this man.

Her climax hit her hard and fast, then lingered. "I love you," she yelled as she came. It felt like Aaron absorbed her trembling with his own body as he took each pleasurable shiver and enhanced it.

"One more," he demanded, the husky timber of his voice setting her off again.

"God, yes!" He drove her to the peak once more and they dove over the cliff together.

Lying on their backs, they were quiet for several moments, both of them obviously lost in thought. The silence was broken by Aaron's stomach growling loudly.

"Guess man cannot live on sex alone," she teased.

"God knows I've tried these past couple of days."

"Are you sure you don't wanna try the all-you-can-eat again? I'll give you yellow."

He groaned. "I don't think I'm ever doing one of those buffet bars again."

She laughed. "Never say never. Room service?"

He turned to face her and nodded. "Yep. I'll call." Moving forward, he placed a brief kiss on her lips.

"I love you, Aaron Dung," she said.

Aaron chuckled. "I love you too, Metal Mouth."

EPILOGUE

"Okay. Quiet down everybody." Sean waited while his family settled into their seats. "That was Riley on the phone. They've just landed at BWI, so if we've timed it right, she and Aaron should be here right about the time the wedding DVD ends. Then we can do this wedding reception thing in style."

A loud cheer accompanied his announcement. Aaron and Riley stayed in Vegas only a week after their initial elopement, and Sean still marveled that somehow that had been enough time for his sisters and sisters-in-law to throw together an impromptu reception. They'd closed the pub and restaurant for the day, decorated the place with white bells, balloons and lots of flowers, rearranged the chairs so they were organized in rows in front of the big-screen TV in the corner. Sean grinned. The flat screen generally broadcast sporting events. This was the first time it had ever been used to show a wedding.

When Sean told Riley what they were organizing, she'd overnighted the wedding DVD and asked him to show it to everyone just prior to the reception. She insisted it would make up for the fact she'd gotten married without the family being present.

He pushed play and then opened the letter Riley had attached. "Riley sent a letter with the video," he explained. "She figures you'll have a lot of questions while you watch. The answers are all in here." He picked up the karaoke microphone and added in a deep, sportscaster-like voice. "I'm Sean Collins, your wedding announcer."

They all laughed. Sean looked around the room, pleased to see that everyone had arrived for the party. He loved the times when the whole family got together. Pop was front and center and beaming from ear to ear. As was becoming a family tradition, there was an empty seat with a white rose on it to mark their mother Sunday's spot.

Keira, Will and their daughter Caitlyn were sitting in the front row with Pop. Keira had just found out last week the baby she was carrying was a boy. Teagan and Sky had flown in from LA late last night and were sharing the second row with Tris and Lane, who were each holding one of their twin sons on their laps. Lily, Justin and Killian were in the third row with Ewan and Natalie, while Chad, Sean's best friend, was sitting next to Sean's girlfriend Lauren in the back row. Both of them were grinning at him and giving him the thumbs-up.

"Who are all those people?" Keira asked as the wedding procession started. "Is that Jo and Trev?"

Sean picked up Riley's letter. "Here. Let me read what she wrote. She says this is her *second* wedding to Aaron. She wanted us to see the DVD of the ceremony she actually remembers."

Pop crossed himself and muttered, "Lord preserve me," as the rest of the family laughed.

"That sounds like our Riley," Tris shouted.

Sean continued reading. "Apparently this was a triple wedding, and just before Aaron and Riley renewed their vows they stood up for Trev and Jo, who renewed theirs also."

"Is that Wayne Newton?" Pop asked excitedly. "She got Wayne Newton to attend her wedding?"

Sean shook her head. "No, Riley knew you'd think that, Pop, so she's written here in all caps THAT'S NOT WAYNE. It's a taxi driver by the name of Johnny Sparks. The third wedding was this Johnny guy marrying some stripper named Bella."

Sean turned and looked at the video. He'd watched it last night so he'd be able to explain who was who to the rest of them. He pointed to the screen. "The blonde woman is the stripper."

"Well, does the taxi driver at least sing?" Pop asked. "I wouldn't mind hearing *Danke Schoen*."

"Nope. Riley says he's tone deaf."

Teagan and Sky burst into laughter at that announcement. "I'll sing *Danke Schoen* for you later, Pat," Sky promised.

"Who's the woman with the purple hair?" Killian asked.

Sean grinned widely. "That's our new kitchen assistant and part-time waitress, Bubbles, the ex-hooker."

Pop leaned closer, trying to get a better look at the woman Riley had talked him into letting work at the restaurant until she got her feet under her. "She looks nice enough. Don't know what the deal is with all that hair."

"Oh Pop," Keira said with a giggle. "I still can't believe you agreed to let her work here."

Pop shrugged. "I dare any of you to say no to Riley once she's made her mind up about something. Besides, she needed to pick her own assistant. God willing she won't fly off the handle and fire her. Ewan's been pulling his hair out trying to find someone to work with her in that kitchen."

"Here, here," Ewan chimed in.

"You know your sister. That girl talked my ear off for nearly half an hour on the phone the other night. In the end, it was just easier to agree."

Riley walked down the aisle in blue jeans and a white T-shirt that said *Viva Las Vegas*, fitting considering they'd gone back to the Elvis Chapel to renew their vows. Aaron was dressed in jeans as well, but his T-shirt said *What Happens in Vegas Stays in Vegas*. The irony of that wasn't lost on Sean as he read Riley's extremely detailed letter regarding their adventures in the neon city.

Bubbles stood beside Riley as maid of honor and

Trev was Aaron's best man. Ewan chuckled when he saw that. "Bet Aaron was thrilled to have Trevor Blankenship as his best man."

Tris grinned. "Guess Trev was a better choice than that Wayne Newton character. Why's Trev so red?"

Sean consulted the letter. "The mob left him in the desert to die without sunscreen."

"Well, that sucks," Tris joked.

Justin leaned forward, squinting at the TV. "Does Aaron have a black eye?"

Sean nodded, loving his role as announcer. He'd always admired his sister's skill for storytelling and it was fun to assume that role in her absence. He had the entire family eating out of his hand, anxious for all the gory details. "Yep, that's a black eye the groom is sporting. He had a run-in with the back of Jo's head during a food fight at the all-you-can-eat."

Natalie looked at Ewan. "You know, I've been to Vegas at least a dozen times and never had any of that shit happen to me."

Ewan shrugged and grinned. "Just another day in my sister's life."

Aaron and Riley said their vows. From the corner of his eye, Sean saw Pop try to discreetly wipe away a tear. When Aaron kissed the bride, Elvis, the minister, started crooning *Teddy Bear* and everyone in the bar applauded. Even with the unusual cast of characters, Sean couldn't help thinking that his sister's wedding had been perfect.

"Is it safe to come in?" Riley asked from the doorway.

Pop led the parade of hugs as the family congratu-lated Aaron and Riley and they, in turn, introduced Bubbles. The evening passed quickly as they ate and drank and danced until the wee hours of morning. Sky sang a montage of Wayne Newton songs in honor of the newlyweds and Riley kept everyone entertained with stories of her Vegas adventure. Trevor and Johanna showed up shortly after they cut the cake and joined the dancing.

The highlight of the party was when Sean carried out the groom's cake Riley had specifically told him to order. Everyone laughed at the cake, which was shaped like two enormous boobs. They all cheered when Aaron bent down to suck the cherry nipple off the top of one.

As the evening began to wear down, Sean sat with his back against the bar, watching as the couples slow-danced. His best friend Chad sat down next to him on one of the barstools. "Another awesome Collins event. Hard to believe the wild-child sister is married."

Sean nodded. "I know. But I have to admit, Aaron is the perfect husband for her."

"He must love the hell out of her to sign on for a lifetime of Riley's quirkiness."

He laughed. "They're gonna be great together," he said as he watched Aaron holding Riley close on the dance floor. It was clear they only had eyes for each other and Sean wasn't sure he'd ever seen his sister look happier.

"You know, this may go down in history as Riley's greatest Saturday Night Special ever.

. . .

THANKS SO MUCH FOR READING! Be sure to check out the entire Wild Irish series.

Come Monday
Ruby Tuesday
Waiting for Wednesday
Sweet Thursday
Friday I'm in Love
Saturday Night Special
Any Given Sunday
Wild Irish Christmas

AND DON'T MISS the next generation, Wilder Irish.

Wild Passion
Wild Desire
Wild Devotion
Wild at Heart
Wild Temptation
Wild Kisses
Wild Fire
Wild Spirit
Wild Side
Wild Night
Wild Embrace
Wild Dreams
Wild Chance

. . .

FANS OF WILD Irish AND Facebook! There's a group for you. Come join the Wild Irish Facebook group for sneak peaks, cover reveals, contests and more! Join now.

BE sure to join my newsletter for a FREE Wilder Irish short story, One Wild Night.

ANY GIVEN SUNDAY

Sean loves Lauren. Chad loves Sean. Lauren loves Sean and Chad.

When an opportunity arises for the threesome to explore their deep desires, they plunge into a sex-filled, emotionally charged ménage. Long-buried feelings are revealed, changing their lives irrevocably.

Whether for better or worse, only Sean, Chad and Lauren can decide.

Excerpt:

"I kissed Lauren this afternoon."

The words flew from his lips more abruptly than he'd intended.

Sean stared at him for a very long, very frozen moment. Then his gaze traveled to Lauren. "He did?"

From the corner of his eyes, Chad saw Lauren nod.

"It was my fault," he added. "She tripped and I

caught her. It was a stupid, impulsive thing to do, but I swear to you, man, it'll never happen again."

Sean rubbed his cheek and Chad stood his ground. It was impossible to know how Sean would respond to anything. Typically his reactions were so unconventional, they left Chad speechless.

This time was no exception.

"You've never kissed her before today?" Sean asked.

Chad shook his head, confused.

Sean looked at Lauren then winked. "Is he a better kisser than me?"

She released a loud breath that betrayed how much confessing to Sean had scared her. Leave it to his friend to break the tension with humor. "Sean," she said.

Sean shrugged. "Sort of surprised it's never happened before this. I mean, you guys have been in each other's faces pretty much night and day for the past six years."

Chad put his hands in his pockets, unsure how to reply. Sean was right. He'd lusted after Lauren for years. Spent at least a thousand nights dreaming of her soft lips…

He needed to get out of here. He wasn't sure how to explain the difference between living in this house versus the apartment he'd shared with Sean, but it was as if his entire life was suddenly moving too fast, like his days were numbered.

Sean and Lauren would get married, move on without him, and he was acting like an ass trying to cling to something that wasn't there to begin with.

He sighed. It felt like a huge part of his life was missing.

"You don't wanna take a swing at me?" Chad asked. "I think if the shoe was on the other foot, I'd pound your ass into the ground."

Sean shook his head. "I'm not mad."

Chad looked at Lauren, who grinned as they both recalled her saying the exact same words a few minutes earlier.

Sean sat down on the couch. "I guess I should be, but I'm not. In fact…" He paused and Chad waited to hear the rest of his sentence.

"In fact what?" Lauren asked.

Sean grinned crookedly. "Naw, it'll sound too weird."

"Say it," Lauren prompted.

"I'm sort of sorry I didn't get to see it."

"What the fuck is wrong with you?" Chad asked, his temper exploding. He'd been kicking his own ass all afternoon, feeling like the world's biggest shit, and now Sean was saying he was sorry he didn't get to see his best friend betraying him.

"Told you it was weird."

Lauren perched herself on the end of the recliner. "Only you would regret something like that." She laughed lightly before sobering. "Sean, I love you. I would never, ever cheat on you. I swear it."

"I know that. And I think if it had been any other guy doing the kissing, you'd be pulling me off him right now as I tried to beat him to a pulp." Sean looked at him and Chad fought to catch a breath at the complete and unquestionable understanding in his friend's gaze. "But Chad's different. He's a part of us."

Sean's words hit him like a blow to the chest and Chad realized two things. One, he wanted to be a part of them. And two—he wasn't.

"I'll pack," he said. "Move out."

"What?" Sean stood quickly, shaking his head. "The hell you will. Didn't you hear what I said? You belong here." Sean looked at Lauren. "Right?"

Clearly Sean was suddenly worried Lauren would be uncomfortable with the current living arrangements.

"Right," she said, so confidently there could be no mistaking her agreement.

They both wanted him to stay. He'd never felt so wanted…and so trapped.

Any Given Sunday is available now.

ABOUT THE AUTHOR

Virginia native Mari Carr is a New York Times and USA TODAY bestseller of contemporary romance novels. With over two million copies of her books sold, Mari was the winner of the Romance Writers of America's Passionate Plume award for her novella, Erotic Research. She has over a hundred published works, including her popular Wild Irish and Compass books, along with the Trinity Masters series she writes with Lila Dubois.

Follow Mari:
www.maricarr.com
mari@maricarr.com